'Well, you've certainly proved a point.'

Sarah raised her eyebrows. 'I have?'

'Yes, I'd practically given up reading my horoscope because it's always wrong, but this morning mine said to expect a special encounter early in the day.' Again the amusement was there in his eyes, but this time the full, finely shaped mouth was also curved into a smile.

'Oh, they are right sometimes,' said Sarah, smiling. 'Take mine, for example — beware flattery from a dark stranger.'

'*Touché!*' Liam murmured.

Dear Reader

Christine Adams's second book, LOVE BLOOMS, shows how the air ambulance service works, and looks at amnesia. Elisabeth Scott's story, set in general practice in the north of England, has Neil's expertise clashing with Sarah's local knowledge. Laura MacDonald looks at trying to go back when people have grown away from each other, and Margaret Barker's Scottish general practice story shows how Ian's understanding helps Heather to cope with her past. We hope you like them.

The Editor

Laura MacDonald lives in the Isle of Wight. She is married and has a grown-up family. She has enjoyed writing fiction since she was a child, but for several years she has worked for members of the medical profession both in pharmacy and in general practice. Her daughter is a nurse and has also helped with the research for Laura's Medical Romances.

Recent titles by the same author:

GYPSY SUMMER
WAITING GAME

A CASE OF MAKE-BELIEVE

BY

LAURA MacDONALD

MILLS & BOON LIMITED
ETON HOUSE   18–24 PARADISE ROAD
RICHMOND   SURREY   TW9 1SR

*First published in Great Britain 1993
by Mills & Boon Limited*

© Laura MacDonald 1993

*Australian copyright 1993
Philippine copyright 1993
This edition 1993*

ISBN 0 263 78094 5

*Set in 10½ on 12 pt Linotron Times
03-9304-48236*

*Typeset in Great Britain by Centracet, Cambridge
Made and printed in Great Britain*

CHAPTER ONE

'PHONE call, Sarah!' called her father from the small room he used as an office.

She paused at the front door, one hand on the latch. 'Who is it?' she mouthed as her father's head appeared round the door.

'Gary.' He smiled as she hurried back down the hall.

She wrinkled her nose at him and took the receiver. 'Hello, Gary?'

'Sarah—hi. Glad I caught you before you left. I wanted to wish you luck on your first day.'

'Thanks, Gary.' Her tone softened and she was suddenly ridiculously pleased that he had remembered.

'Are you nervous?' he asked.

'Yes, I am a bit. I've never worked on a gynae ward before.'

'You'll be all right. Cool, calm and collected, that's my Sarah. Oh, there was just one other thing.'

'Oh. . . ?'

'Yes.' He hesitated and she knew what was coming before he said it. 'I'm afraid I won't be able to make tonight. There's a squash match. . .and now I'm in the league. . . Sarah, are you still there?'

'Yes, Gary, I'm still here.'

'I'm sorry—I know you wanted to see that film,'

said Gary. 'Maybe you could get someone else to go with you. Anyway, I must dash; I'm going into Bournemouth with Dad today. I'll give you a ring tomorrow.'

Sarah stood for a moment staring at the receiver before replacing it, then she stepped from the office and caught sight of her father's face as he hovered anxiously.

'Anything wrong, love?' he asked.

She shook her head. 'Not really. Gary can't see me tonight; he's playing squash.'

Her father looked uncomfortable. 'Well, I suppose now that he's in the league. . .' He trailed off.

'Yes, quite, Dad,' Sarah said briskly, but as she climbed into her car a few minutes later she found herself thinking that if it hadn't been squash it would most probably have been rugby, or football or one of the many other sporting activities that Gary was involved in. She was beginning to think she was seeing even less of him now that she'd moved back to their home town than she had while she'd been away doing her training.

She pulled away from the kerb with a backward glance at the three-storeyed, gabled house where she had spent her childhood. In those days it had been a flourishing guest-house, but now, with dwindling numbers of summer visitors to the Dorset seaside town, her parents had converted it into flatlets.

It was a bright morning in October, the early mist had lifted, the cobalt-blue sea was as calm as a millpond and the distant white cliffs shone in the autumn sunlight. Sarah drove along the deserted esplanade, then took the steep cliff road into town, her pace slowing as she joined the early morning traffic at a large roundabout. The Royal County Hospital, a sprawling stone building, stood at the far side of the town, and fifteen minutes later she drove in through the main entrance and took the signposted route to the gynaecology wing.

After parking her car in the staff car park she walked across the tarmac, arriving at the large double entrance doors at the same moment as a man who appeared to be in a great hurry. He wore a brown cord jacket and a white shirt open at the neck, and his dark hair looked tousled. When he saw her, however, he stopped dead and with a gallant flourish allowed her to precede him.

'Thank you,' Sarah nodded, and in that single moment noticed that his dark eyes seemed full of amusement, while his mouth remained serious.

In the foyer he strode purposefully forward while she paused, hesitating, then as he stepped into the lift he turned and, seeing her indecision said, 'Where do you want to go?'

'Gynae.'

'Quickly, then.'

She rushed forward, just catching the doors before they closed, while he caught hold of her elbow to steady her. They were both laughing as he pressed the button for the second floor, then he turned to her, and this time there was curiosity in the dark eyes.

'I haven't seen you before. You must be staff— you couldn't possibly be a patient at this ungodly hour.' The soft Irish brogue was instantly identifiable.

'Quite right. Sarah Bartrum — it's my first day.'

The lift stopped, the doors opened and they stepped out into a cream-painted corridor.

'Liam O'Neill.' He held out his hand and Sarah found hers clasped in a firm, warm handshake. As he released her hand he stood for a moment looking at her, then he said, 'Well, you've certainly proved a point.'

She raised her eyebrows. 'I have?' They began to walk down the corridor.

'Yes, I'd practically given up reading my horoscope because it's always wrong, but this morning mine said to expect a special encounter early in the day.' Again the amusement was there in his eyes, but this time the full, finely shaped mouth was also curved into a smile.

'Oh, they are right sometimes,' said Sarah, smiling at his approach. 'Take mine, for example — beware flattery from a dark stranger.'

'*Touché*,' he murmured, then stopped, and leaning forward, tapped on a partly open door. 'Where are you, Sister? I can't start my day without a smile.' He winked at Sarah as the door was pulled open, revealing a middle-aged woman in dark blue sister's uniform, a look of mock severity on her features.

'Dr O'Neill, you're quite impossible, you know that? The patients are all in love with you and you break my nurses' hearts — it's no good, you'll have to go.'

'Sister, you've wounded me to the quick; I'll have

to creep away and lick my wounds, but let it not be said that I shirked my duty. I rescued this fair maiden in the lift and deemed it my responsibility to deliver her safe and sound to you lest she fell into the clutches of some evil registrar.' He turned and, taking Sarah by the hand, moved her forward into the office.

Sister raised her eyebrows. 'Staff Nurse Bartrum, I presume?'

Sarah nodded, still smiling, while Liam O'Neill leaned on the door-handle, a hopeful expression on his face. 'Is there anything else I can do to be of assistance? Maybe show your new member of staff around?'

'No, thank you, Dr O'Neill,' said Sister firmly.

'It's no trouble. . .'

'Goodbye, Doctor, I'm sure you have work to do.' As she closed the door, Sister turned to Sarah with a laugh.

'He really is the limit. He's kissed the Blarney stone and no mistake. I'm sorry; you must think we're all completely round the bend.'

'It makes a nice change from my last hospital,' Sarah told her. 'Everyone there was grumpy first thing in the morning; sometimes you were lucky to even get a "Good morning".'

'Oh, I'm not saying we don't get a few mornings like that here. But Dr O'Neill is always the same.'

'He seemed very nice,' said Sarah, glancing back at the door.

Something in her tone must have sounded wistful, for Sister glanced sharply at her. 'He's a bit of a one for the girls,' she said, and there was a warning note in her voice.

'Oh, don't worry about me,' Sarah laughed. 'I'm spoken for.'

'Well, that's a relief — at least I won't have another broken heart to patch up.' Sister rolled her eyes. 'Anyway, let's get down to business. It's Sarah, isn't it? I'm Sister Moore, Pat to the staff.' She turned to the desk, put on a pair of glasses and picked up a folder. 'Shall we just go through your details? I was on leave when you came for your interview.' She opened the folder and glanced through the contents. 'You're twenty-two? You did your training at St Joseph's and this is your first job in gynae?'

'Correct on all three counts,' said Sarah.

'Why did you leave St Joseph's?'

'I wanted to return here to my home town. My family and my boyfriend live here, and I was finding it very expensive living in the London area.'

'Fair enough. So are you living with your parents?'

'More or less. Our house has been converted into flats, and I'm renting one of them.'

'Very convenient.' Pat Moore laughed. 'Home life and independence.'

Sarah nodded. 'Yes, it suits me for the time being.'

'You spoke of a boyfriend — is he a local boy?'

'Yes. Gary Jones — his father owns the plant hire firm.'

'Oh, yes, I know them. Gary's a bit of a golden boy of sport, isn't he?'

'You could say that.'

'Any sign of wedding bells?'

Sarah smiled. 'Maybe — one day. We've been going together since high school.'

'Ah, I see. So why did you choose gynae?'

'I particularly enjoyed gynae during my training.'

'Well, we're pleased to have you. I hope you'll be happy with us. Now if you'd like to get changed I'll find someone to show you round. . .but it won't be Dr O'Neill!'

In the staffroom Sarah changed into her uniform, proudly fastening the dress with her staff nurse's belt and the silver buckle her parents had given her when she qualified. Her dark hair was almost shoulder-length and she had already caught it back in a prettily woven plait that sat neatly under her cap. When she was ready she glanced in the mirror above the washbasin; clear hazel eyes stared back at her above a short straight nose, generously curved mouth and a rounded, determined chin. Critically she checked the light make-up she wore for work, then after fastening her fob-watch she straightened her shoulders, smoothed down her dress and walked out on to the ward.

By this time the rest of the early morning shift were assembling in Sister's office for report. As Sarah appeared in the doorway Pat Moore looked up from her desk. 'Ah, here she is. This is our new staff nurse — Sarah Bartrum. It's her first time on Gynae, so I'd like you all to be as helpful as you can.'

The other nurses all looked at Sarah and nodded or smiled, and one of them, a girl with flaming-red hair, beckoned her to a chair. As Sarah sat down she said, 'Hi, I'm Ria Burrows.'

Sarah only had time for a quick hello and to notice that Ria was a staff nurse like herself, before the night sister came into the room to give her report to the day staff. The report gave a detailed account of each patient. Most appeared to be recovering from operations, and the report stated at what stage they were in their recovery, what medication they had been given and other details like whether they'd spent a comfortable night or if they'd been restless.

After report the day team went straight into action with their daily routine of serving breakfast, which would be followed by bed-making and bed-baths for those patients who weren't mobile.

As Sarah hovered uncertainly Sister Moore called Ria back into the office. 'Ria, before you start could you please show Sarah around?'

'Sure.' Ria's face with its smattering of freckles broke into a grin. 'I'd be glad to.'

Sarah followed her out of the office — then almost fell over her as the other girl stopped dead, looking first right, then left.

'I was just wondering where to start,' she explained. 'You see, the ward is divided into two — pre-op and post-op. We have eight beds in each. Come on —' she turned right '—we'll start in pre-op, then graduate into the recovery section, just as the patients do.'

Sarah was surprised to find six empty beds in the pre-op section, especially when Ria went on to tell her that it was a very busy ward with two consultant surgeons operating almost every day.

'I can see you're wondering about these empty

beds,' she chuckled when she caught sight of Sarah's face. 'We have six admissions later today, and these two ladies——' she indicated the other two beds '—had their operations two days ago and will be moving down into Recovery after the doctors' ward round.'

They moved out of the pre-op ward and down the corridor again, where Ria pointed out the staff kitchen and rest-room, the sluice, patient bathrooms and the store-rooms, taking special care to show Sarah the cardiac arrest trolley, the emergency box and the fire exits before they entered the post-op ward.

This ward was big, light and airy. All eight beds were occupied, the patients in various stages of recovery from a variety of operations. When Sarah and Ria arrived two enrolled nurses and an auxiliary were serving breakfast, and several of the patients looked up with interest on seeing a new face.

'Ladies, this is Staff Nurse Bartrum,' explained Ria. 'Be kind to her; it's her first day on the ward.'

There were smiles and hellos from the patients, and as they left the ward Ria said, 'It's a very happy ward, as you'll have noticed.'

Sarah nodded. 'Have you been here long?'

'Five years.'

'You must enjoy it.'

'I do. As I said, it's a happy atmosphere. You see, with most of these ladies, once their operation is over they recover quickly. There are exceptions, of course; we have in fact a couple of single-bedded wards for anyone who's really sick or terminally ill.'

'Do you get many of those on Gynae?'

'A few. Then of course there are the emergencies.' Something in Ria's tone made Sarah throw her a quick glance. 'Oh, yes, Gynae's notorious for emergencies. Just when you think you have a clear ward for five minutes, it's not unusual to get three emergencies on the trot. You know the sort of thing — pelvic pain, ectopic pregnancies and abortions — anything prior to the twenty-eighth week of pregnancy. After that they go to Obstetrics, of course.'

Then, glancing round, Ria said, 'Well, I think I've shown you everything. As soon as breakfast is clear perhaps you'd like to help with bed-baths for those two ladies down in the other ward.'

Gradually Sarah was absorbed into the busy ward routine, and after she'd helped with the bed-baths of the two patients who were both recovering from abdominal hysterectomies she went back to the post-op ward. She found two enrolled nurses and an auxiliary engaged in bed-making.

'Can I help?' she asked the nurse who was working on her own.

'Oh, yes, thank you.' The girl was small, plump and pretty with fair curly hair. 'I didn't think we were going to get through before ward round,' she said as they stripped a bed. 'I'm Lucy, by the way, and that's Kath over there, and Tina. You're Sarah, aren't you?'

'Yes.' Sarah launched straight in with the bed-making, pausing only to nod to the other two nurses.

Lucy chattered away while they worked, asking Sarah where she had trained and about working conditions in her last hospital, then suddenly Sarah became aware that the other two nurses were giggling and she heard Kath, the auxiliary, say, 'Is he on duty today?'

Both girls had stopped what they were doing and were craning their necks to see into the corridor. Lucy looked over her shoulder at them, then turned back to Sarah, and as she passed her a set of clean sheets she rolled her eyes.

'What is it?' Sarah tried to see what they were looking at, but the corridor seemed to be empty.

'They're waiting for the doctors,' said Lucy under her breath, with a glance at the patient whose bed they were making and who was sitting in a chair reading her morning newspaper. 'Tina's waiting to see if Dr O'Neill's on duty this morning. He's our senior houseman; he's Irish, and very, very dishy. Tina, among others, is madly in love with him, and on the days he isn't on duty she goes into a sulk. I think we could be in for a day of that today, because someone said they thought he wasn't here.'

'Oh, but he is,' said Sarah.

'How do you know?' Lucy looked at her in surprise.

'I saw him earlier—when I arrived, in fact. We came up in the lift together.'

'But how did you know who he was?'

'I didn't—he made himself known to me.'

'That sounds like Dr O'Neill,' said Lucy drily, while Tina, at the mention of his name, turned from the bed she was making.

'What was that?' she frowned.

'Sarah was just saying,' explained Lucy, 'that Dr O'Neill is on duty this morning.'

Tina stared at her suspiciously and Kath gave a snort. 'Good God, she's only been in the place five minutes and she knows the movements of the doctors!'

'Oh, it wasn't like that. . .' Sarah began to explain, but was prevented from saying more as there was a noise in the corridor and Sister appeared with a white-coated entourage, while the patient who had een engrossed in her newspaper looked over her asses at Tina.

'You'll be all right today, love. Here comes that ctor you fancy,' she said as she climbed laboriously ck on to her bed.

Sister was wheeling a trolley containing each patient's records, and as she pulled the curtains round the first bed Lucy said quietly to Sarah, 'The tall grey-haired man is Mr Hunter—he's one of our consultant gynaecologists, the Asian gentleman is Dr Patel, the registrar, the SHO, as you know, is Dr O'Neill. The blond junior doctor is Philip Taylor, but I can't remember the other one's name.' She glanced round. 'I think we're just about finished; let's get these dirty sheets out of the ward before Sister gets down here.'

Sarah, pushing the dirty linen trolley, followed Lucy down the ward, and noticed that Tina was fussing around the washbasins, obviously determined to stay in the ward.

As they reached the beds by the door the curtains were whisked back and the group around the bed moved out, blocking the gangway. Sarah, with her trolley, almost collided with one of the white-coated figures who stepped straight into her path, then when he turned to apologise she found herself for the second time that morning staring into the same pair of dark eyes.

The surprise in his expression was quickly replaced by the amusement that she'd seen there before, and spontaneously she found herself smiling back.

'Ah, Nurse Bartrum,' he said. 'So how's it going? How are they treating you?'

To Sarah's confusion, before she had the chance to answer, Mr Hunter turned to see who Dr O'Neill had spoken to and peered at her over his half-glasses.

It was Sister Moore who came to her rescue. 'It's Nurse Bartrum's first day with us, Mr Hunter, and quite honestly, Dr O'Neill, I don't think she's had time yet to say how it's going, and we certainly haven't had the time to treat her badly. . .yet,' she added with a mock severity that even produced a thin smile from Mr Hunter.

Liam O'Neill grinned, completely unperturbed. Sarah noticed the cord jacket had been replaced by a white coat and that he was now wearing a tie. It also looked as if he'd made an attempt to tame his tousled hair. 'Well, you just let me know when they start treating you badly.' He winked at Sarah before disappearing behind the next set of curtains.

As she turned to close the doors behind her and make her escape the last thing Sarah saw in the ward was Tina's expression, one of angry suspicion.

By the time they reached the sluice Lucy was chuckling.

'What's the matter?' asked Sarah.

'It looks as if you've put Tina's nose out of joint,' Lucy replied.

'Well, I certainly didn't intend to,' protested Sarah. 'Maybe I should explain to her.'

'I shouldn't bother — Tina can be a bit of a pain in the neck at times, especially where Liam O'Neill is concerned.'

'Even so. . .if she and he have something going between them it's understandable that she —— '

'But they haven't,' interrupted Lucy. 'That's the whole point. It's only wishful thinking on Tina's part.'

'And on Dr O'Neill's?'

'He's his usual charming self, but he's like that with everyone — you wouldn't believe the hearts he's broken since he's been here, what with those gorgeous eyes and that fatal Irish charm.'

'Sister more or less said the same,' Sarah agreed drily, then added, 'Well, here's one heart he won't be breaking.'

'Mine neither,' said Lucy as they left the sluice-room. 'I'm married. How about you?'

'Oh, I'm not married yet, but I do have a steady boyfriend, so I won't be susceptible to Dr O'Neill's charm.'

'Well, he'll certainly use it to try and get you involved with his fund-raising schemes for the hospital's Body Scanner Appeal.'

'Oh, I don't mind helping with that,' said Sarah.

'Just as long as that's all he tries. Now what have we to do next?'

'Coffee, I think, then Ria will probably want you to help with dressings. Then after lunch we have the new admissions.'

CHAPTER TWO

THE morning continued with an emergency admission—a girl of fifteen who had been taken ill in the school swimming-pool with acute, left-sided, low abdominal pain. She had been seen by her GP, then brought to hospital in an ambulance accompanied by a teacher. She appeared frightened and distressed by the pain.

Ria admitted her to the ward, then when she returned to the office where Sarah was making out drug charts she said, 'Would you go and sit with her until the doctor comes to examine her?'

Sarah nodded. 'Of course. What's her name?'

'Kelly. Oh, and put a "Nil by Mouth" sign above her bed until we know whether or not she's to go to Theatre.'

The curtains were drawn around Kelly's bed, and when Sarah parted them she found the girl wide-eyed, flushed and very tearful.

'Hello,' she said cheerfully. 'My name's Sarah; I've come to keep you company until the doctor comes to see you.' Leaning across the bed, she inserted the card that Ria had given her in the slot above the head-rail.

'What's that?' The girl tried to twist around.

'Only a card to tell everyone that you mustn't have anything to eat or drink.'

'Why?' Kelly demanded suspiciously.

'We always do that just until the doctor's examined you and decided what he's going to do.'

'Will I have to have an operation?' The girl's eyes widened in fear and she winced suddenly with renewed pain.

'I don't know. You may do,' said Sarah truthfully. 'But again that depends on what the doctor says.'

'Has my mum come yet?'

'She hadn't a moment ago. Has someone let her know you're here?'

The girl nodded. 'Yes, my teacher was going to ring her at work—I don't know if they'll let her come, though; she works on the check-out at the supermarket.'

'Oh, I'm sure they will when they know what's happened,' said Sarah comfortingly, then as the curtains parted again she looked up. 'Here's the doctor now,' she added as Dr O'Neill appeared.

'Hello, Kelly,' he said with a brief glance at Sarah, 'and what have you been up to?'

'I was swimming and I got a pain—here.' Kelly pointed to a spot beneath the blankets, and Dr O'Neill moved forward to sit on the bed after indicating for Sarah to stay.

She watched as gently he examined the girl, all the while talking to her, calming her, in his soft Irish tones, asking her about school, her hobbies, her pets, whether or not she had a boyfriend, which made her giggle, and then, when he had finished, standing up and stepping back just as Ria looked through the curtains to say that Kelly's mother had arrived.

'I expect you'll be wanting to see your mum, Kelly?' he asked, and when she nodded he went on, 'Well, I'll tell you what we're going to do. Nurse Bartrum and I will leave you for a little while to chat. We'll go off and have a think about what we're going to do with you. Maybe we'll get another doctor to come and look at you, but you won't mind that, will you?'

Kelly shook her head, the fear and suspicion gone from her eyes now, so much so that when her mother appeared a few seconds later the girl seemed so relaxed it was as if she was reassuring the worried woman instead of the other way round.

Sarah followed Dr O'Neill to the office. 'You did a good job with Kelly,' she commented.

He looked up from reading Kelly's case notes in surprise. 'In what way?'

'Well, she was very agitated.'

'And who wouldn't be?' He shook his head. 'The poor little thing was frightened, what with the pain and everything.'

Sarah remained silent, but she couldn't help wondering whether his show of compassion had been put on to impress her because she was new, or whether he was always so considerate. She decided from her previous experience of hard-pressed housemen that the latter was highly improbable, but she thought she'd take note in future and find out.

'I want the registrar to have a look at her,' he added, and picked up the phone on the desk.

'What do you think is wrong?' she asked.

'I suspect an ovarian cyst — oh, hello, Julie,' he spoke into the mouthpiece. 'Could you page Dr Patel, please?'

He replaced the receiver and looked at Sarah. 'If it is, we'll probably have to operate.' Then, glancing at his watch, he said, 'Have you been to lunch yet?' She shook her head. 'Good. I'll see you in the canteen; I want to ask you about the Scanner Appeal.' The phone rang and he picked up the receiver again. 'Ah, Rajiv? Can you come up to Gynae?'

He went on to explain Kelly's symptoms to the registrar, and while he was still talking Ria came into the office. 'Sarah, would you go to lunch now, please? Then you'll be back before the new admissions arrive,' she said.

When Sarah sat down in the staff canteen ten minutes later she found that her head was buzzing with all she'd seen, heard and tried to absorb that morning. But as with any new ward it had been a challenge, and she'd enjoyed it.

She was about to tuck into her salad when she was joined first by Lucy, then seconds later by Liam O'Neill.

'He wants me to help with his Scanner Appeal,' said Sarah with a smile as he set his tray down on their table.

'I warned you, didn't I?' Lucy sighed. 'No one escapes. Are you aware of what you're letting yourself in for?'

'I'm not agreeing to anything until I know exactly what it entails,' said Sarah firmly.

'It'll probably be a sponsored birdwatch, just you and Liam in a hide in the middle of nowhere, so watch him,' said Lucy darkly.

'Now would I suggest such a thing?' Liam looked hurt, but Sarah noticed that the laughter still lurked in his eyes.

'Yes, Liam, that's just the sort of thing you would suggest,' said Lucy, then added, 'Go on, admit it.'

'Well, maybe it would have been once, but I'm a reformed character these days; haven't you noticed?'

'No, Liam, I haven't.' Even Lucy was laughing now.

'So what's your next fund-raising event?' asked Sarah. She knew from reading the local papers just how much interest there was in the Scanner Appeal and how much money had already been raised, not only through the hospital but by other local organisations.

'The next event is later this month,' he said, and there was no disguising the enthusiasm in his voice as he went on to explain, 'It's to be a twenty-mile sponsored walk followed by a barbecue and firework display on the beach.'

'Twenty miles?' Sarah stared at him aghast.

Lucy grinned. 'Do I take it from that you're not the sporty type?'

Sarah shook her head. 'No, sorry, I'm not. I never have been—I was even barred from the school netball team because I always dropped the ball.'

'Sounds a bit like me,' chuckled Lucy. 'Snakes and

Ladders is the most energetic game I've played. Still, never mind; we'll just have to start training, won't we?'

Sarah still looked dubious, then Liam said, 'We're having a meeting tonight in the social club to discuss the details. See you both there.'

'Hold on a minute,' said Lucy. 'I'm not sure if I can make it, and I expect Sarah's going out with her boyfriend.'

Liam turned his head and for a moment his dark eyes met Sarah's. This time the amusement was missing. 'Are you?' he asked.

Sarah shook her head. 'No, as it happens, I'm not. Not tonight, anyway.'

'So you'll come, then.' It was almost a statement, as if there could be no doubt that she would come.

'I. . . I suppose so. . .' She glanced at Lucy. 'How about you?'

'Oh, all right, then, but I can't stay for long.' Lucy drained her cup, then glancing at her watch said, 'Lord, look at the time. We must be getting back — Ria will be going spare.'

Sarah pushed her tray away and stood up. Liam looked up at her, and as the light caught his features she noticed that his eyes, which she had thought of as merely being very dark, were in fact flecked with green, while his features were strong and clearly cut, the nose straight with slightly flaring nostrils, the mouth sensual and the jaw firm and decisive.

Suddenly she became aware that he knew she was studying him, and in confusion she looked away, to escape his amused enquiring gaze.

When they returned to the ward it was to find that Kelly was being prepared for Theatre and the first of the afternoon admissions had arrived.

Because Ria was with Kelly, Sister instructed Lucy to do the patients' afternoon observations — temperatures, pulse-rates, fluid charts and blood-pressure checks — then she told Sarah and Tina that she wanted them to admit the new patients.

'There are six admissions, all for Theatre tomorrow,' she explained. 'One's an elderly lady, Mrs Woodmore, who's been suffering from severe stress incontinence; she's to have a bladder repair. Then there's a laparoscopy; in this case it's an investigation on a young woman who's finding difficulty in conceiving. There's a possibility that her fallopian tubes may be blocked. We have two hysterectomies for tomorrow's list — one's being performed for a lady with fibroids and the other on a patient who unfortunately has been diagnosed as having a carcinoma of the cervix.' She glanced up at Sarah and Tina as she spoke, then continued, 'There's also one termination of pregnancy and one cone biopsy. You'll take three patients each, enter all their details, explain their operations to them and ask them if they have any worries or problems. Then when they've undressed and their relatives have gone the doctor will come and see them individually and you'll remain with each patient while she's being examined. Later this afternoon the surgeon and the anaesthetist will come and talk to them and we'll explain tomorrow's pre-op routine, but first let's get the admissions under way.'

Sarah's first patient was a lady in her forties, a Mrs Baines, who was to have a hysterectomy for the discovery of several large fibroids in her uterus which had been causing heavy bleeding. After Sarah had checked her name, address, date of birth, next of kin, religion and the name of her GP, she attached a plastic identification bracelet to her wrist. She then went on to ask about previous illnesses and operations.

'I had my tonsils out when I was a child,' explained Mrs Baines, 'and when I was in my teens I had my appendix out.'

'So you've had an abdominal operation—you know a little about what to expect.'

Mrs Baines pulled a face. 'I remember not being able to sit up because it was so sore.'

'Yes, you will be sore for a few days,' admitted Sarah, 'but we'll give you something to help control the pain, and it'll all be worth it in the end.'

'Yes,' agreed Mrs Baines. 'It'll be nice not to have those dreadful periods every month. I was feeling so tired and run-down all the time.'

'That's right. Now do you have any worries, anything you want to ask me, either about the operation or any problems at home? I see your husband is your next of kin. Will he cope all right while you're out of action?'

'Oh, yes, he used to be a cook in the Navy, so I've no worries on that score. . .but there was just one thing, Nurse. . . I expect you'll think this sounds silly, but I don't want to take my wedding-ring off. Will I have to?'

'No, Mrs Baines, not if you don't want to. It's a general rule that patients remove all jewellery before going to Theatre, but lots of patients like to keep a wedding-ring on. We'll cover it for you with a piece of sticky tape. Now is there anything else you want to ask me?'

'I don't think so, Nurse.'

'Well, if you'd like to come with me I'll show you to your bed, you can get undressed, then your husband can come and see you before he goes home.'

While Mrs Baines was getting undressed Sarah went back to the examination-room to admit her second patient. This was a young woman in her early twenties who was to have a cone biopsy of the cervix following several positive cervical smear results.

Her attitude seemed brash, almost defiant, but Sarah sensed that deep down she was very frightened. Her name was Donna, she was a single parent with two small children by different fathers, and she had just started a new relationship with a man of nineteen. She told Sarah these details as if she was trying to evoke some reaction, but when Sarah remained impassive she lapsed into a bored silence.

'Where are your children at the moment?' asked Sarah.

The girl shrugged, tossing back her shaggy dyed hair to reveal an ear pierced several times and fitted with studs and gold sleepers. 'Social services got them.'

'I see — well, you shouldn't be in here for too long,' said Sarah, then when she went on to ask if

Donna had any other questions or worries the girl
replied,

'Where can I have a smoke?'

'Smoking isn't allowed on the ward,' explained
Sarah, then when she saw Donna's mutinous
expression she added, 'There is a day-room where
you're permitted to smoke, but it isn't advised,
especially before an operation.'

'Yeah, I know all that, but I can't go without me
fags.'

While Donna was getting undressed Sarah looked
at her list and saw that her third patient was called
Val Smith and that she had come into hospital for a
termination of pregnancy. Somehow she expected a
young girl, a teenager perhaps, but the patient who
came into the examination-room was in her forties.

As Sarah took her details she realised that the
patient was tense and nervous. She told Sarah that
she had three children, all grown up, that she and
her husband had been going through a very stormy
patch and that when she'd missed first one, then a
second period she had imagined she'd started her
menopause. Her GP had sent her for a pregnancy
test which had proved to be positive.

'It was the last straw,' she said bleakly. 'My
marriage just couldn't stand another child. I don't
think my sanity could either.' Her hands shook as
she fumbled in her handbag for a tissue.

'Do you have any immediate worries about coming
into hospital, or about the op itself?' asked Sarah
gently.

'Only that anaesthetic makes me very sick.'

'I'll make a note of that on your file, but do tell the anaesthetist when he comes up to see you. Anything else?'

'Oh, yes, just one thing. I don't want the other women in the ward to know. . .'

'That's quite all right; there's no reason for anyone to know, and you'll be going home later tomorrow in any case.'

'Supposing someone asks me outright? Some people can be very nosy.'

'Yes, I know.' Sarah smiled. 'In that case you simply say you're having a D and C—no one will be any the wiser, I assure you. Now if you'd like to go and get undressed, do a specimen of your urine, and the doctor will be along shortly to examine you.'

'What for? I've been examined. . .there won't be any doubt?' queried Mrs Smith.

'No, this will simply be a routine examination to make sure you're fit for the anaesthetic.'

When Sarah returned from taking Val Smith to the ward she found Tina outside the examination-rooms. She smiled at her. 'Have you finished your three?' she asked.

The girl nodded but didn't smile back, and Sarah remembered the silly incident in the ward that morning. She bit her lip and turned away.

'Here's the doctor now,' Tina said suddenly, then she frowned, and when Sarah turned to see why she saw that Dr O'Neill was accompanied by one of the younger housemen who had done the morning ward round.

'Are you ready for us, ladies?' Liam put the

question to them both, but his gaze lingered on Sarah.

It was Tina who replied, however. 'Yes, thank you, Doctor. Nurse Bartrum has seen her patients over there and I've seen mine in here.' She moved forward as she spoke as if she expected Liam to follow her.

Instead he turned to the younger houseman. 'Philip, as you're fairly new here, you go with Nurse Mills, she'll show you the ropes, and as Nurse Bartrum is new I'll go with her. Otherwise we could have a serious case of the blind leading the blind, and we don't want that, do we, Nurse Bartrum?'

'We don't indeed,' murmured Sarah, then, catching sight of Tina's murderous expression, she dived back into her examination-room.

She knew Liam was watching her, and to cover her confusion she began bustling around straightening things that didn't need straightening, then when she really couldn't find anything else to do she turned and found him leaning against the couch, his arms folded. The usual humorous glint was in his eyes.

'Are you ready, Nurse?'

'Ready?'

'Yes, have you finished your tidying up?'

'Oh. . .yes, yes, I think so.'

'Well, in that case do you not think it might be a good idea to call a patient?'

To her horror, it dawned on her that that was what he had been waiting for. Hot with embarrassment, she fled from the room, cursing herself for her stupidity. Whatever must he think of her? She, a staff nurse now and supposedly competent with all routine procedures, and she had kept him waiting a good five or six minutes while she had fussed over jobs that hadn't needed doing in the first place. But she had only done so because he had confused her. Taking a deep breath, in an effort to pull herself together, she walked on to the ward and asked Mrs Baines to come with her.

'Is it to see the doctor?' Mrs Baines, resplendent in a new pink quilted dressing-gown and fluffy slippers, walked with Sarah down the short corridor.

'Yes — don't worry. He only wants to listen to your chest and ask a few questions.'

'Oh, I'm not worried. Is he nice?'

'Er — yes, very nice,' replied Sarah as at that moment Tina passed by with one of her patients and pointedly ignored her.

Ten minutes later Sarah escorted a chuckling Mrs Baines back to the ward.

'A bit out in your judgement there, weren't you, love?' said the patient.

'What do you mean?' Sarah looked at her curiously.

'Very nice, you said. Very nice? He was gorgeous! If they're all going to be like him, I shall enjoy my time in here, and that's a fact. Did you hear what he said about my not looking nearly old enough to have a married daughter?'

Leaving Mrs Baines to tell the woman in the next bed about her encounter with Dr O'Neill, Sarah pulled back the curtains around Donna's bed.

Dressed in a thigh-length, grubby T-shirt with a

Hell's Angels motif on the front, Donna was lying full length on her bed smoking a cigarette. Her heavily mascaraed eyes defiantly met Sarah's and she calmly leaned across to her locker and stubbed out the cigarette in an empty saucer.

'The doctor's ready to see you now, Donna, if you'd like to come with me.'

With a bored sigh the girl swung her long legs off the bed and stood up.

'Do you have a dressing-gown?' Sarah glanced around, noting the empty peg behind the bed.

Donna shook her head and pushed her feet into a pair of worn canvas shoes before starting off down the ward, leaving Sarah to catch her up.

As they entered the treatment-room and Dr O'Neill looked up from reading Donna's case notes, Sarah decided he would have to go into overdrive if he was to charm this particular patient.

Donna remained uncooperative while she was being examined, her answers to Dr O'Neill's questions abrupt and flippant, then when he was listening to her chest she coughed, and he frowned.

'How many do you smoke a day, Donna?' he asked.

She shrugged. 'I don't know.'

'How many, Donna?' he persisted quietly.

'About twenty. . .it varies. . .whatever I can afford.'

'You have quite a bit of congestion on your chest — don't you think it might be a good time to be thinking of cutting down while you're in hospital?'

'Oh, don't you start; she's already had a go at me.' Donna jerked her head in Sarah's direction.

'I see your children are being cared for while you're with us,' Liam said quietly, and when Donna merely nodded in response he glanced quickly through her details again, then said, 'Do you understand what you're having done tomorrow?'

'Yeah, having a bit cut out to see if I've got anything nasty. Right?'

'Yes, Donna, that's right, more or less. The surgeon will take a tiny cone-shaped wedge from your cervix for testing. Now, do you have any questions?'

'Yeah. When can I go home?'

Dr O'Neill glanced at her case notes. 'I should think, all being well, the day after tomorrow.'

'What do you mean, all being well?'

'Exactly what I say. If all goes well with your operation and you're feeling fit, you should be discharged the day after tomorrow.'

'Right.' Donna stood up. 'Can I go now?'

Dr O'Neill nodded, and, scuffing her feet, she walked to the door. 'Oh, Donna,' he called, and she stopped but didn't look back, 'Watch the smoking!'

She didn't answer and, not waiting for Sarah, she opened the door and walked out into the corridor, leaving the door open behind her.

Liam O'Neill raised his eyebrows at Sarah. 'Thank you, Nurse. Would you like to bring——' he glanced at his notes '——Mrs Smith in now, please?'

Sarah, deciding that even the charm of Liam O'Neill couldn't be guaranteed to win over everyone, found she was more than impressed with the way he dealt with Val Smith. He talked to her for a long time, adding to the counselling she had already received, so that when Sarah returned her to the ward she was in a much calmer frame of mind than when she had been admitted.

When all the ladies were back in the ward, Ria, as senior staff nurse, came to tell them the routine preceding their operations, while Dr O'Neill went to see Kelly, who had just come back from Theatre following the removal of an ovarian cyst.

As Sarah was so new to Gynae she listened carefully as Ria told the six new patients that they would not be able to have anything to eat or drink from midnight, and that when they woke in the morning they were required to give urine specimens. She went on to explain that they were each to take an unscented bath and to make sure they had removed all jewellery and all traces of make-up and nail varnish before putting on a theatre gown.

'Now, ladies,' Ria concluded, 'if you'd all please lie on your beds, as both the surgeon and the anaesthetist will be along shortly to visit you.'

As Sarah followed her back to the office, Ria glanced over her shoulder and said, 'How did you get on with the admissions?'

'All right, I think.'

'Did you have Dr O'Neill with you?' she asked, then when Sarah nodded she said, 'I suppose they all fell for him?'

Sarah grinned. 'All except Donna.'

'Oh, you wait; he'll have her eating out of his hand before he's finished.'

'Doesn't he have any faults, for heaven's sake?' sighed Sarah.

'I've heard he has a quick temper, when he's roused.' Ria grinned, then added, 'But somehow I should think that would only make him more attractive.'

Sarah smiled, but found she was inclined to agree with Ria.

CHAPTER THREE

WHEN her shift ended Sarah decided she would go home and have something to eat before returning to the hospital social club for the meeting about the Body Scanner Appeal.

She parked her car outside Linfield House, let herself in and was just climbing the stairs to her flat when her mother called out to her from the down-stairs apartment where she and her father lived.

'Come and have a cup of tea, Sarah; I'm dying to hear how your first day went.'

She found her mother in her kitchen setting out flowered china mugs and a plate of biscuits. Grate-fully Sarah eased herself on to one of the kitchen stools. 'Oh, it's good to sit down,' she sighed.

'Busy, was it?' Diane Bartrum smiled sympatheti-cally, and poured boiling water into the teapot. She was small and dark with only slight touches of grey in her hair to give away the fact she was twice her daughter's age.

'Yes, it's certainly all go on a gynae ward,' said Sarah, helping herself to a digestive biscuit as she realised how hungry she was.

'Never mind, you can take it easy this evening. Dad said Gary had a squash match,' Mrs Bartrum explained when Sarah looked up.

'Yes, he has, but I have to go back to the hospital.'

'Good heavens, they have got you working hard.' Her mother looked up in surprise.

'Oh, it's not work. I've been roped into a meeting for raising funds for the Scanner Appeal.'

'Well, that's certainly a good cause.' Diane Bartrum poured the tea, passed a mug across the breakfast bar to Sarah, made herself comfortable on another of the stools, then with her head on one side she said, 'Well, come on; tell me all about it.'

'To tell you the truth, I've been so busy I haven't really had time to think,' admitted Sarah.

'All right, then, first impressions.'

'First impressions. . .' she mused. 'Let's see — oh, well, my very first impression was of a slightly crazy but very charming doctor whom all the rest of the staff seem to treat as if he were God's gift to women.'

Her mother smiled. 'Sounds dangerous. What about the rest of the staff — what were they like?'

Sarah considered, sipping her tea appreciatively. 'Very nice really. I palled up with a girl called Lucy, and I think I shall get on well with the senior staff nurse, Ria Burrows.'

'What about the sister?'

'Oh, she was great; she has a sense of humour too, which makes all the difference. . . There was only one girl, Tina, who I didn't get off to a very good start with, but — well, there's always one, isn't there?'

'But you do think you're going to like it?'

Sarah was aware that her mother was looking anxiously at her and she knew she'd had her doubts about her returning to her home town to work after being away for the last three years. 'Yes, Mum, I think so,' she replied. 'It's a very busy ward, and I like that. I'll just have to give it time.' She glanced up then and frowned. 'Are you all right?'

'Me?' Her mother looked up quickly.

'Yes — you look tired.'

'I suppose I am.' Diane sighed. 'I shall be glad to get away now. It's funny, but when we first booked this holiday I didn't really want to go; now I can't wait.'

'You and Dad really need this break,' said Sarah slowly. 'The worry of this place has taken its toll on you both over the last couple of years.'

Her mother nodded. 'Talking of this place, are you sure you'll be all right while we're away?'

Sarah sighed and smiled. 'Oh, Mum, of course I will. It's not even as if I'm alone in the house, after all.'

'That's true — three flats are occupied now. There's only one to fill, and I've advertised that in the local paper.'

'There's a noticeboard in the canteen at the hospital,' said Sarah thoughtfully. 'Write out another advert and I'll take it in tomorrow. Nurses are always after accommodation.'

'Yes, I'll do that.' Her mother finished her tea and stood up. 'So when are you seeing Gary again?' she asked.

Sarah shrugged. 'I'm not sure really. He said he'd ring tomorrow, and I suppose I'll have to go and watch his rugby match on Saturday.'

'I was talking to his mother yesterday in the

hairdresser's. She's delighted you've come back, Sarah.'

I bet she is, thought Sarah, as her mother went off to the office to write out her advertisement. She'd always had the feeling that Gary's mother didn't really like her, that in some way she felt as if Sarah wasn't good enough for her son.

As she climbed the stairs to her flat Sarah found herself remembering that there had once been a time when she herself might have thought that. A time when at high school it had seemed impossible that Gary Jones, hero of the sports field and champion swimmer and athlete, should notice her, Sarah Bartrum, lowly fifth-former and hopeless at any form of games. But notice her he had, they had started dating, and somehow their relationship hàd even survived her being away the three years while she had done her training.

During this time Gary had gone to work for his father in the family plant hire company, and it had been as if he had automatically assumed that she would return home when her training was over. Sarah herself, if she was honest, was still faintly amazed at how the relationship had lasted.

She loved Gary, who was tall, fair-haired and handsome, and she was prepared to put up with the hours she spent watching him take part in his various sporting activities, helping him to celebrate when he won and dreading the times he lost, when he would sink into a depression from which it was difficult to lift him.

Her flat was on the first floor and had views of the

sea from her sitting-room, which also had french doors opening on to a tiny balcony. She knew she had been lucky to get this particular flat, but it and the adjoining one had been the only vacant two in the house when she had returned home from London a few weeks previously.

Putting her bag and car keys down on to the table, she walked into her bedroom and tossed her coat on to the bed. Initially she'd had several doubts about returning to her family home to live—not because she didn't get on with her parents—they'd always been close—but because she had so enjoyed her newly found independence and because her parents had always inclined towards over-protectiveness.

It was, however, all turning out far better than she had feared. The flat, freshly decorated in soft pastel tones, was delightful, and her parents seemed to be allowing her all the independence she needed, even turning a blind eye on the occasions when Gary stayed the night.

She had chosen her own soft furnishings in rich printed oriental-style fabrics, added plants—trailing ivy, shiny-leaved yuccas and kangaroo vines—covered the bare walls with travel posters and bright gouache prints and filled shelves with books and her music centre. Within a couple of weeks she had stamped her personality on the flat. And now even her job looked promising; in fact, thought Sarah as she prepared a light meal, life really was beginning to look very good, in spite of her earlier misgivings.

Later she showered and changed into mulberry-coloured cords and a cream patterned sweater, shook

her hair loose around her shoulders and left the
house to drive back to the hospital.

There seemed to be numerous activities under way
when she arrived at the social club, and she tried
several rooms to find where the meeting was taking
place. In the first room a group of porters were
playing snooker, in the second some of the nursing
staff were engaged in a frantic table-tennis tourna-
ment, while in the bar those who weren't standing
around drinking were playing darts. In the end Sarah
asked the barman where the meeting was for the
Body Scanner Appeal.

'Oh, they're out the back; you can come through
this way if you like—save you going all round the
building again.' He indicated a door at the back of
the bar, then pulled up the counter flap, standing
aside so she could squeeze past him.

'Thank you.' Sarah lifted her hand to knock on the
door, but the barman grinned and opened it. She
found herself in a small passage lined with barrels
and crates with another door facing her. The barman
opened this second door and, addressing someone
inside, said, 'Another recruit here for you, Doc.
She'd got lost; I think she needs taking care of.' He
turned and winked at Sarah, then with a flourish
gestured her into the room.

She was greeted by a sea of faces, and to her
dismay realised she had entered the room from the
front. A man seated at a table in front of the full
rows of chairs had turned to see what was happening,
and when he saw Sarah he got to his feet.

With a jolt she saw it was Liam O'Neill. But then

it would be, she thought miserably as the barman shut the door behind her — after all, it was Liam who had apparently called the meeting. For a moment she felt a sense of isolation and almost wished that the barman had come in with her, then she felt her cheeks grow hot as the occupants of the room stared at her with interest.

'Sarah!' Liam was smiling now. 'I was beginning to think you couldn't make it. We've only just started, so you haven't missed much. Please take a seat.' He indicated one empty chair on the end of the second row, and as Sarah thankfully sank down she caught sight of Tina Mills' smirking face. Tina was sitting in the front row directly in front of Liam's table.

For the first five minutes Sarah didn't hear a word that Liam said as she sought to regain her composure, but as the meeting progressed she found herself becoming involved, and in the end she marvelled at how Liam persuaded even the most reluctant among the gathering to do exactly what he wanted.

The main topic under discussion was the sponsored walk and the barbecue. The walk was open to all hospital staff and they were free to collect as many sponsors as they could.

'Tina, can I leave the distribution of the sponsor forms to you?' said Liam. 'And perhaps you could compile a list of names and addresses of everyone wishing to take part. Yes? Good, oh, and Lucy, will you arrange the en-route refreshments?' Liam smiled and glanced at his notes. 'Now what else is there? 'Oh, yes.' He glanced up and his gaze fell on Sarah.

'Sarah, would you organise the sale of the tickets for the barbecue and firework display?'

'Of course. I take it the barbecue is open to friends and relatives?' asked Sarah.

'Yes, but only ticket-holders will be admitted, so it's up to you to sell as many as you can — and while we're on that subject, Philip, could you contact the fire brigade? They've already agreed to control the firework display, but we weren't able to give them the exact date before.'

And so it went on, until everyone had a job to do and Liam brought the meeting to a close.

As Sarah stood up she saw Tina heading purposefully for Liam's table, then Lucy touched her arm.

'Time for a quick drink?'

'OK, Lucy, yes.'

They went through to the bar, where Lucy bought two glasses of wine and carried them to a quiet corner alcove.

'You've had quite a first day, haven't you?' She grinned at Sarah as she sipped her drink.

Sarah nodded. 'You could say that.'

'As if a first time on Gynae weren't enough, you've been well and truly roped in to Liam's crazy fund-raising.'

'Oh, I don't mind really; it's all in a good cause after all, and he does seem to put his heart and soul into it.'

'Yes, he does that,' Lucy agreed. 'Before this he was raising money for the children's ward — it was incredible. He raised thousands, and I don't doubt when this is over he'll find something else.' She glanced up. 'Oh, talk of the devil.' Then, smiling sweetly, she moved along the seat. 'Hello, Liam, we were just talking about you. Come and sit down.'

'Dare I ask what you were saying?' Liam's query as he sat down was directed at Sarah.

'Only how incredible it is how much money you manage to raise for charity.'

He shrugged. 'There's nothing incredible about it — you simply appeal to folks' better nature.'

'That may be so, but it still takes an awful lot of time and effort,' Sarah pointed out.

'Well, all I can say is that it keeps him out of mischief,' said Lucy. 'Just think what he'd be getting up to if he had all that time on his hands.'

They carried on discussing the walk and other ways they could raise money for the scanner, then Liam drained his glass and stood up. 'Let me get you girls another drink — what will it be?'

'Not for me, thanks.' Lucy got to her feet. 'I have to go; Colin's mother's coming to supper, but you stay, Sarah.'

'Oh, no, really, I'm driving,' Sarah began as Liam picked up her empty wine glass.

'Then I'll get you a fruit juice, or a Coke — what would you like?'

'Oh, all right, an orange juice, then.'

'I'll be away, then, Sarah,' said Lucy with a grin. 'See you tomorrow, bright and early.'

While Liam went to the bar Sarah watched as Lucy left the club. She had a vague feeling of unease, a feeling that told her she shouldn't really be sitting in the social club drinking with Liam O'Neill. Then as she watched him walk back across the floor to their alcove she asked herself where the harm was. It was only a simple drink, after all, and they would no doubt only be discussing the sponsored walk.

He set two glasses of orange juice carefully on the table, and Sarah noticed his finely shaped hands, the sensitive fingers and the slightly squared nails. He was wearing the same jacket he'd been wearing that morning when they'd first met, but tonight he was also wearing a black polo-necked sweater and denims.

Silently he raised his glass to her, and for one wild moment she thought he was going to say, 'To us.'

When he remained silent she raised her glass and said, 'Here's to the sponsored walk.'

He nodded. 'I'll drink to that.'

As they set their glasses down he said, 'Thank you for coming to the meeting. It was good of you, especially as it was your first day with us.'

'I didn't mind really; in fact I quite like fund-raising. I used to do a bit during my training.'

'And where was that?' Liam turned his head and there appeared to be genuine interest in his dark eyes.

'St Joseph's in London.'

'Did you like it there?'

'Very much.'

'So why the change?'

She hesitated, then shrugged. 'Personal reasons . . .family mainly.'

'Your family live here?'

'Yes, I was brought up here.'

He looked surprised. 'So it's a case of a return to the home town.'

'Is that so surprising?' she queried.

'Not really, I suppose,' he reflected. 'It's just that I couldn't somehow imagine returning to my home to work.'

'And where exactly is home?' She turned slightly and saw that his expression had softened.

'Connemara. It's one of the most beautiful parts of Ireland, but my home is in a small village in a very rural area.'

'So where did you do your training?'

'Dublin.'

'Do you miss Ireland?'

He nodded. 'Sometimes I do. I come from a large family—there were seven of us. My mother had me down for the Church, but I knew I wasn't cut out to be a priest.' The humour was back, replacing the wistfulness that had been in his eyes while he'd been talking of his home. 'I'm not sure she's ever forgiven me,' he concluded.

'Oh, I'm sure she has,' said Sarah. 'She must be proud that you're a doctor.'

'Maybe she is.' His smile implied that he knew she was. 'And how about you? Have you always wanted to be a nurse?'

'Always,' she replied firmly. 'Even when I was a little girl I used to cover everyone with bandages. It seemed the most natural thing in the world to do my training after leaving school.'

'I know what you mean. It was the same with me. I always knew I would be a doctor.' Liam looked down at his hands. 'I always had this urge to heal things, to make things whole again.' He fell silent for a moment, then glancing sideways at her again he asked, 'Did you have any particular reason for choosing gynae?'

'No, not really. I just happened to be looking for a job, and this one came up.'

'Do you think you'll like it?'

'Yes, I think so. It's a very busy ward, isn't it?'

He nodded. 'You can say that again.'

'Are you aiming to specialise in gynae?' Sarah asked.

'That's the general idea. There's a junior reg. post coming up next year when Li Chang goes home. I'm intending to apply if I can get Roland Hunter's approval.'

'Are you assisting Mr Hunter in Theatre tomorrow? I understand we have a full list.'

'I am.' Liam glanced at her empty glass. 'Can I get you another?'

'No, thank you, I really must be going.'

He stared at her for a long moment as if he was searching for the right words to ask something. 'Sarah. . . I was wondering,' he said at last, 'would you come out with me some time?'

She swallowed, for her immediate reaction had been to say yes. She had a feeling it would be very pleasant to spend some time with Liam O'Neill, but she knew that was out of the question. 'I'm sorry, Liam. I'd love to, but I already have a boyfriend.'

'Ah, yes,' he said, and there was a note of regret in his voice, 'I remember. Lucy mentioned your boyfriend earlier. It's a shame; I feel we could have a lot in common.'

Sarah nodded, agreeing with him, almost certain that they would indeed have much in common, but suddenly she was lost for words. She stood up, picking up her bag and her car keys.

'Local, is he?'

Sarah looked down sharply and saw that Liam hadn't attempted to move and was apparently intently studying a beer mat, rolling it between his fingers.

'I beg your pardon?'

'Your friend? Local man, is he?'

'Yes—yes, he is.' He stared up at her as she answered, and this time she was unable to interpret the expression in his eyes, but he appeared to be waiting for her to say more. 'His name's Gary Jones; his father owns the plant hire company in town—you may have heard of them.'

'So have you been going together for long?' He neither admitted nor denied having heard of the hire company.

Sarah nodded. 'Yes, we have. Ever since high school, in fact.'

'And do you have a lot in common with him?'

She stared at him. 'Well, yes, I suppose we must have. . .' She faltered, then frowned. 'Look, I'm sorry, but I really must be going.'

'Are you meeting him?' Liam stood up and began to follow her out of the club.

'No, not tonight; he's playing squash.'

'So why the hurry?'

'I have to get home, that's all. It's been a very long day.' She glanced over her shoulder at him, but his expression was inscrutable. He walked in silence with her to her car.

'Thanks for the drink,' she said as she unlocked the door and slipped into the driving seat.

'See you tomorrow,' he said softly.

Her last glimpse of him was in her driving mirror as she drove out of the car park, and he stood watching her, silhouetted in the light from the club.

Sarah felt strangely elated as she drove home. Surely it couldn't be because Liam O'Neill had asked her out? If what the rest of the staff had said was anything to go by he seemed to make a habit of chatting up new members of staff and then going on to break their hearts.

Well, he would certainly be out of luck as far as she was concerned, she thought as she drew to a halt outside Linfield House. She definitely wasn't about to succumb to his charm. That he was charming and very attractive she would not dispute, and yet — she paused before climbing out of her car and staring out to sea where a large orange moon was caressing the horizon — there had been something about him that had led her to believe he wasn't a womaniser. But maybe that was where he was clever; maybe he gave that impression to gain a girl's confidence.

She slipped out from behind the wheel and locked her car door, and just before she entered the house she told herself that it really didn't matter one way or another what Liam O'Neill said or did. She didn't care — after all, she had Gary.

CHAPTER FOUR

THE following morning by eight-thirty the six ladies who were to go to Theatre had bathed and were lying on their beds dressed in white theatre gowns. Mrs Baines and an elderly woman, Mrs Woodmore, who was to have a bladder repair, were the first on the list and had already been given their pre-med injections.

Sarah had drawn the curtains round their beds so that they could relax in privacy and had just gone back to check on them when she paused to have a word with Kelly, who was recovering from her operation.

'How are you feeling this morning, Kelly?'

'My tummy's very sore.'

'Yes, it will be for a while. Move around in the bed as much as you can and you'll find it'll soon get easier.'

'Sarah,' called Ria from the end of the ward, 'the porters are here for Mrs Baines—can you give a hand, please?'

Sarah had already been told that she was to accompany some of the patients to Theatre that morning, and she hurried to Mrs Baines's bed, where she found two porters positioning the theatre trolley.

'You're going for a ride now, Mrs Baines,' said Sarah, noting that her patient already looked sleepy

51

as the poles were inserted into the canvas stretcher ready to lift her on to the trolley.

'That'll be nice. Shall we have a quick trip down to the shops?' Mrs Baines managed a smile and a wave to the other patients as she was wheeled out of the ward, then as they proceeded down the corridor she looked up at Sarah. 'Will that nice doctor be there?'

'Which one do you mean?' asked Sarah, knowing full well to whom she was referring.

'The Irish one with the lovely eyes. . .' murmured Mrs Baines sleepily.

'I don't know; you'll just have to wait and see,' said Sarah, surprised and faintly annoyed that her own pulse had started to race at the mention of Liam.

When they reached Theatre they were admitted to the preparation-room, where the anaesthetist was waiting to receive the first patient of the morning. Sarah leaned forward and briefly squeezed Mrs Baines's hand. 'I'll be back to get you very soon,' she said. 'When you wake up, you'll be back in the ward.'

She had turned to leave when the theatre doors opened and a figure in a green gown appeared. A pale blue cap covered his hair and the lower part of his face was hidden by a mask, but as he looked towards Sarah there was no mistaking his eyes.

'Thank you, Nurse Bartram,' he said, then, leaning over the trolley, he added, 'And a very good morning to you, Mrs Baines. You're looking very lovely this morning. Where shall we go?'

As Sarah pulled the door shut the last thing she
saw was the smile on Mrs Baines's face. Maybe Liam
O'Neill was full of blarney and flattery, but he
certainly did the patients good, she thought as she
returned to the ward.

Her next task was to give Donna her pre-med.
Sarah had wondered what frame of mind she would
find the girl in that morning, but she wasn't really
surprised to find a very subdued Donna lying on her
bed. All the defiance of the previous day had van-
ished, and clad only in her white theatre gown, with
her face scrubbed clean of make-up, she looked
vulnerable and very young.

'What you gonna do?' She looked suspiciously at
the small tray in Sarah's hands.

'I'm going to give you something to help you to
relax,' explained Sarah, drawing the curtains around
the bed.

'A fag would do that,' muttered Donna.

'Would you like to turn over on your side?'

'Why? I don't want no needles.' The girl sounded
alarmed now.

'It won't hurt, really it won't,' said Sarah briskly
as she pulled up Donna's gown and swabbed a small
area on her thigh ready for the injection of Pethidine.
'How old are your children, Donna?' she asked
casually.

'One and three.'

'Just a little scratch now. . .' Swiftly Sarah admin-
istered the injection. 'Are they boys or girls?'

'Girls. . . Samantha and Michelle.'

'What pretty names. That's all now; I'll leave the

curtains round and you can rest.' Sarah was about to leave when Donna suddenly raised her hand as if she wanted to say something. 'What is it, Donna?'

'What happens next?'

'You'll rest for a while, then you'll be going down to Theatre.'

'Will I be asleep before I go in there?' Fear flickered in Donna's eyes.

'Yes, don't worry. Before you know, it'll all be over and you'll be back here in bed,' Sarah assured her.

'Will you come with me?'

'Yes, I expect it will be me,' said Sarah.

'I don't want that ginger-haired one — she's a cow,' said Donna, and the aggressive look was back on her face.

'No, she isn't,' said Sarah firmly, 'she's very nice.'

'I still want you to come with me.'

'Well, I'll see what I can do — on condition that you get some rest.'

Donna nodded, and Sarah left her, noticing as she passed Kelly's bed that the girl had just had a basket of fruit delivered.

'So who's a lucky girl?' she smiled.

Kelly looked up. 'It's from my form at school — look, they've all signed this card.' She held up a huge card with two cute teddy bears on the front.

'Nurse!' Sarah turned as one of the ladies who'd had a hysterectomy two days previously called out to her. 'Would you help me to the bathroom, please?'

'Of course. I'll just take this tray away, then I'll be right back for you.'

For the next hour or so Sarah carried on with all the daily routine tasks that had to be fitted in around the operating list. Then a call came from Theatre to say they were ready for the next patient and that Mrs Baines was ready to return to the ward.

Sarah escorted Mrs Woodmore down to Theatre, noting as she did so how calmly and philosophically the seventy-eight-year-old woman seemed to be facing the prospect of surgery.

This time there was no sign of Liam in the prep-aration-room, and Sarah realised that she had in fact subconsciously been looking for him and was faintly disappointed when he wasn't there. A few minutes later, however, when she went to the recovery-room to collect Mrs Baines, she found him giving the surgeon's notes to the recovery staff nurse.

He glanced up as she went into the room. 'Ah, here you are, Sarah. Mrs Baines is fine—no compli-cations. I was just telling Staff Nurse Richards here that it'll be you selling the tickets for the barbecue. Helen——' he turned to the staff nurse '—this is Sarah Bartrum.'

The two girls stared at each other, then Sarah gave a cry of pleasure. 'Helen! Oh, how marvellous! I didn't know you worked here.'

'Sarah—why, Sarah Bartrum! I haven't seen you for ages, not since we went off to do our training. This is a nice surprise.'

'I take it you two know each other.' Liam stood with his hands on his hips looking from Sarah to Helen.

'Yes, we were at school together,' said Sarah

happily. 'Then I went to London and Helen went to Salisbury.'

'Not married, are you, Sarah?' asked Helen.

Sarah laughed and shook her head. 'No, not yet.'

'You're not still going out with Gary Jones?' asked Helen in surprise.

Sarah nodded, and the two girls spoke for a couple more minutes about their families, but when Sarah turned to include Liam she found he had gone.

She returned Mrs Baines to the ward, keeping a careful watch as she did so on her breathing and on the saline drip. She then gave the surgeon's report to Sister together with the medication that had been written up for Mrs Baines; Pethidine for pain and Temazepam as a sedative, then she returned to the patient to check her pulse and blood-pressure.

Sarah had been delighted to find Helen Richards working in Theatre. The two girls had been through the sixth form together, studying for exams at the same time, and while Sarah had been dating Gary Helen had been going out with Gary's friend Chris. She hadn't had time to ask Helen whether she was still seeing Chris, but as she turned her concentration to the busy ward routine once more she decided she and Helen would have to get together and talk over old times.

The theatre list continued throughout the morning. Ria took a patient down for a laparoscopy and brought Mrs Woodmore back to the ward, then Sarah took Donna down.

She was pleased to see that the girl looked drowsy, and although she remained silent on her journey down the corridor when they reached the preparation-room and Sarah reassuringly patted her hand she suddenly clutched Sarah's hand and held it tightly.

'What is it, Donna?' Sarah whispered, leaning over the girl so that the porters wouldn't hear.

'I'm scared,' she muttered.

'Don't be. There's nothing to be afraid of, really there isn't. You'll be asleep in a few minutes and you won't know anything about what's going on.'

'It's that I'm scared of.' Donna's eyes were dark with fear.

'What, not knowing what's going on?' Sarah frowned and out of the corner of her eye she saw that Liam had come into the room and was quietly watching them.

'No, not that. It's another needle, isn't it? What puts me to sleep?'

Of course, that was it, thought Sarah as she remembered the girl's fear over her pre-med. She glanced up at Liam and saw that he'd heard and summed up the situation.

He moved forward into Donna's line of vision and, taking her other hand, looked down at her. 'Hello, Donna. Let's get this over as quickly as we can, shall we?'

She frowned, then she must have recognised him in spite of his mask and gown, for she managed a grin. 'Yeah, then I can get back for a fag,' she said.

'That sounds more like the Donna I met yesterday. Thanks Nurse Bartrum.' He nodded at Sarah as with a final squeeze she extricated her hand from Donna's and left the room, feeling that Liam was the best person to dispel any fears that Donna had. It seemed incredible that her fear of needles far outweighed any worry over the possible results of her cone biopsy. Sarah wondered if in fact, while the girl seemed to understand the nature of her operation, she understood the implications of a biopsy.

When Sarah returned from her morning coffee-break both Donna and Val Smith were back in the ward and sleeping off the effects of the anaesthetic.

The rest of the day was taken up with the post-operative care of the theatre patients. They all had to be washed and changed from the operating gowns into fresh nightclothes, analgesics had to be given, fluid outputs measured and catheter bags checked for the three ladies who'd had major surgery, together with half-hourly observations of pulse and blood-pressure on them all.

As Sarah was nearing the end of her shift she heard the sound of weeping coming from Val Smith's bed. Quickly she pulled the curtains and, leaning over the bed, she put her arm round the woman's shoulders.

'I'm s-sorry, I didn't mean to make a fuss.'

'You have a good cry, Val,' whispered Sarah. 'It'll do you good. Here, have a tissue.' She passed a box across the bed, and Val took a hankie and blew her nose.

'It's not that I changed my mind or anything; I knew it was for the best, but. . .but. . .' Val gulped and couldn't continue.

'It's a perfectly normal reaction; don't try and suppress it.'

Sarah sat with Val for some while, then when she had calmed down a little she left her to rest and returned to the office, where she found that Liam had arrived with Mr Hunter.

The consultant had changed his theatre greens for a white coat which he wore unbuttoned over a dark suit.

'Everyone all right, Sister?' he asked.

Pat Moore looked quickly through her pile of case notes. 'No real problems, Mr Hunter,' she replied. 'But maybe you could have a quick look at Mrs Woodmore. Her blood-pressure dropped rather low post-op.'

'Very well.' He followed her from the office, leaving Liam alone with Sarah.

He didn't speak immediately, and Sarah found herself searching for something to say, knowing instinctively that he was thinking of the previous evening when he had asked her out. She sought desperately for anything to break the silence, which had become embarrassing. She began fiddling with some notes and charts on the desk, but with each second that passed she became more and more aware of the man at her side. Then just when she thought she was going to be forced to mumble some excuse and escape from the room he broke the silence.

'Is Donna all right?'

She nodded, relieved that his question hadn't been on a personal level. 'Yes, she's asleep.'

'And Mrs Smith?'

'She was very tearful just now.'

'That's understandable. I'll go and have a word with her before she goes home.' There was another awkward silence, then Sarah looked at her fob-watch. 'It's time I was going home too.'

By this time Liam had sat himself on the corner of the desk and was barring her way to the door. To get past him she would have to brush against his legs. She hesitated.

'Don't let me stop you,' he remarked casually. 'No doubt you'll be in a hurry to get out with the boyfriend tonight.' He moved, but only slightly, and she was still forced to squeeze past him, and it was while she was very close, while her legs were pressed briefly against his, that he reached out and caught her hand.

Startled, she looked at him, but the protest died on her lips as she saw the expression in his eyes. This time the amusement was missing, this time there was an intense look, a look that sent a thrill coursing through her veins. Then without releasing her hand he said, 'Unless of course you've changed your mind, and you're coming out with me tonight.'

She shook her head. 'No, Liam, I haven't changed my mind. I won't be coming out with you tonight, or any night.'

'That's a bit harsh, isn't it?' He leaned towards her and she caught a scent, a mixture of his aftershave and the unmistakable maleness of him. 'What have I done to deserve such finality?'

'Liam. . .' She swallowed. 'I told you ——'

'I know,' he interrupted, holding up his hands as if

to ward her off. 'You said—it's the boyfriend.' He moved even closer then so that his face was only inches from her own. 'But I wonder if this guy knows how lucky he is? Does he, Sarah? Does he appreciate you?'

'I don't know what you mean. . .' It was as if she was mesmerised and quite unable to look away from those wicked dark eyes. Then she was saved by the sound of Sister returning. Casually Liam stood up, drawing away from her in the same movement, so that when Sister came into the room it simply looked as if they'd been discussing a patient. Sarah seized the opportunity to go, and fled from the room without another glance in Liam's direction.

Gary phoned her that evening as he had promised, asked how her job was going, then before she had the chance to go into too much detail went on to ask whether she would be at his rugby game at the weekend. She agreed, because she knew he liked to have her there on the touchline, boosting his ego, cheering his team on to victory and then afterwards joining the other wives and girlfriends in the pub to help the team either celebrate or drown their sorrows. When she finally got round to asking what he was doing that evening she learnt that because his league had won their squash match they had gone forward to the next heat, which started that night.

'Why don't you come up to the sports centre and watch?' he asked her. 'We could go for a drink afterwards.'

'No, Gary, I don't think so. I'll give it a miss

tonight. I'll see you on Saturday.' She replaced the receiver and sat staring at the phone for a few minutes, then on impulse she flicked through the directory and found Helen Richards's number.

Half an hour later she was in her car driving towards Helen's home on the outskirts of the town.

Helen herself opened the door of the tiny semi-detached red brick cottage. 'Sarah, this is nice. Come on in.' She led the way into a small sitting-room.

'I hoped you wouldn't mind, but I thought you'd probably have other plans at such short notice,' Sarah told her.

Helen shook her head. 'No, nothing that can't wait. Alan's on duty tonight.'

'Alan?' Sarah raised her eyebrows, and Helen laughed.

'Yes, Alan Protheroe. I don't think you've met him.'

'Oh, so you're not still seeing Chris. . .?'

'Good Lord, no.' Helen laughed and ran her fingers through her short blonde hair. 'That was over years ago. Soon after we left school, in fact. I think we simply outgrew each other when we got out into the real world. No, there've been a couple of others since Chris, then I met Alan and I just knew that was the real thing. We're getting married next year.'

'That's marvellous, Helen. Congratulations.' Sarah was surprised to feel a sudden pang of envy. 'Is Alan in the profession?'

'No, he's a policeman. But in a way that's very compatible with nursing—we understand each other's shifts and that sort of thing. Now, let me get you a coffee, then we can have a good gossip — we've so much to catch up on.'

Moments later Helen came back into the room with two mugs of coffee. 'I was surprised to hear that you and Gary were still together,' she said, handing one mug to Sarah, then settling herself in a big armchair and tucking one leg beneath her. 'However did you cope while you were away training?'

Sarah shrugged. 'Oh, we managed. I came home some weekends and sometimes Gary came up to town.'

'He's still very involved in sport, isn't he? I keep seeing his name in the local paper.'

'Yes, very.' Sarah sighed and set her mug down on a small coffee-table.

Helen glanced at her sharply. 'That sounded as if it's a bit of a drag.'

'Did it?' Sarah reflected. 'I didn't mean it to really. I should know Gary by now. Sport's the driving force in his life; he'll never change. I expect when he's too old to play he'll watch, so if I stay with him I shall have a lifetime of it.'

'Do you think you will?' asked Helen curiously. 'Stay with him?'

'I expect so. We've survived this long. . .' Sarah trailed off, then changing the subject she said, 'How long have you been at the hospital?'

'Six months.'

'Do you like it?'

Helen nodded. 'Yes, although all the changes are a bit hard to come to grips with. How about you? Do you think you'll like Gynae?'

'I will if I can stand the pace,' Sarah laughed, 'but if every day's going to be like today I doubt if I'll last a week!'

'Pat Moore's sister up there, isn't she?'

'Yes, she seems nice.'

'And how about your SHO?' asked Helen.

'Dr O'Neill? What about him?'

'What do you think of him?'

'He seems OK.' Sarah tried to sound casual, but she was aware that at the mention of Liam's name her heart had started to beat faster. 'Why do you ask?'

'He seemed rather taken with you today.'

'Isn't he like that with any new face?'

'Is he?' Helen raised her eyebrows.

'That was the impression I got from the other girls on Gynae.'

'Well, they probably know him better than I do, but I get the opposite impression.'

'What do you mean?' Sarah stared curiously at Helen, waiting for her to go on.

Helen took another mouthful of coffee. 'Oh, I don't know — I may be wrong, but I felt it was the women chasing him and that he wasn't particularly interested in anyone, until today when he realised I was a friend of yours and he wanted to know more about you.'

'Good heavens, what did you tell him?' Sarah felt her cheeks grow pink.

'Oh, not a lot,' Helen shrugged. 'Only about us going to school together, that sort of thing.'

'You must admit he piles on the charm. Several of the staff warned me about him.'

'I don't know that he does,' mused Helen, 'pile on the charm, I mean. I think that's just his manner. You watch him; he's like it with everyone and, let's face it, he's a damn good doctor.'

'I agree,' Sarah nodded, remembering how Liam had been with Donna and the other patients on the ward.

They changed the subject again after that and talked of their families, mutual friends they'd had at school and the different conditions they'd each experienced during training, and just before she left Helen invited Sarah to a party that she and Alan were holding at the weekend.

'It's to celebrate us finally naming the day,' she laughed.

'Thanks, I'd love to come,' Sarah told her.

'Good—oh, and bring Gary, of course. It'll be nice to see him again after all this time.'

It had been nice to see Helen again, Sarah reflected as she drove home, nice to catch up on all their news and talk over old times, but after she'd reached Linfield House and was preparing for bed it was the conversation they'd had regarding Liam O'Neill that was uppermost in her mind.

CHAPTER FIVE

As THE week went on Sarah became more and more involved in her new life. At home she helped her mother to shop and to prepare for her three-week holiday in Thailand. It was to be the trip of a lifetime for her parents, celebrating their silver wedding anniversary which had fallen earlier in the year. There had at one time been some doubt as to whether they would actually be able to go — business had been bad and the debts had piled up, but gradually things had picked up. The flats had attracted permanent residents instead of just holiday trade, and then just two days before they left her mother told her that her father had had an enquiry for the final flat.

'I'm so glad, Mum.' Sarah hugged her mother. 'Now you can go off and enjoy your holiday and not worry about anything — not even me,' she added when she saw her mother's expression. 'I'm fine, really I am. I have Gary, I shall be seeing him at the weekend, and I've made lots of new friends. It's been great meeting up with Helen again and I'm really enjoying my job.'

It was true, she really was enjoying her job on Gynae, her interest growing with every passing day. By the end of the week, of her first list of admissions she had seen first Val Smith go home, then Donna, who fortunately had been found not to have cervical cancer after all, and then Kelly.

Donna had been back to her old aggressive self by the time she left the ward, but she did manage a goodbye for Sarah. As they watched her saunter down the corridor to join her boyfriend who had come to meet her, Ria said, 'Well, Liam might not have had her quite eating out of his hand, but I'll tell you one thing.'

'What's that?' Sarah threw her a curious look.

'She stopped smoking while she was here.'

Mrs Baines and Mrs Woodmore continued to improve and were counting the days to when they too could go home, and throughout the week there were of course other admissions, more operations and several emergencies.

Once Sarah had learnt the routine she came to love the pace, the constantly changing faces and the rapid recovery enjoyed by the majority of the patients who came on to the ward.

The only slight niggle of unease during those early days in her new job came in the shape of the SHO, for as time went on it became increasingly obvious to Sarah that he constantly contrived to be where she was.

For a while it bothered her—after all, she wasn't free to encourage him—but he did nothing to offend her, and secretly she had to admit she found his presence pleasant, almost exciting, to such an extent that if a lunchtime passed without him appearing or he was absent when she made a trip to Theatre she was disappointed. Gradually, almost without her realising it, she was subconsciously looking for him.

Just before the weekend the tickets arrived from the printer for the barbecue. Liam brought them to her during her coffee-break in the Gynae staff rest-room.

'Here they are, at last.' He handed over four packages. 'Now you can start selling.'

'I'll take them to the canteen at lunchtime,' said Sarah. 'I should be able to get rid of a few there.'

'Yes, and if I were you, I'd take them to Helen's party. People are usually in a good mood at parties.'

Sarah had been about to put the packages into her bag, but she paused at his words and looked up at him. 'Are you going to Helen's party?'

'Of course. As far as I can make out she's cramming half the hospital into that little house of hers.'

Sarah swallowed and began rummaging in her bag. The idea of Gary and Liam meeting was suddenly very unappealing. Feeling Liam's eyes on her, she became flustered and dropped some of the contents of her bag on the floor.

He knelt down and retrieved two of the packets of tickets, a lipstick, comb and some letters and papers for her, and as he handed them over he said, 'Well done; I see you have your sponsor form.'

'I'm not too happy about it,' she mumbled, stuffing everything back into her bag.

'Why ever not?' Liam stood up, and when she glanced up she saw he was smiling.

'I'm not even sure I can manage ten miles, let alone twenty,' Sarah confessed.

'Ah, I can see we'll have to do some training,' he said.

'Good idea,' said a voice, and when Sarah looked round she found Tina standing behind her. She wondered how long she had been there. 'Why don't you organise some training sessions, Liam?' Tina went on. 'I could help you if you like.'

'Hmm, yes, maybe I will.'

He wandered off then, but leaving Sarah even more aware of Tina's antagonism towards her. Miserably she wondered if all the staff were aware of the attention Liam was paying her.

Sarah was working an early shift on Saturday and had planned to go straight to Gary's rugby game when it had ended. She said goodbye to her parents before she left for work because they would have left for the airport before she returned.

It was a fairly quiet morning on the ward with no theatre list, post-op care of the previous day's theatre patients and only one emergency admission. This was a patient in her thirties sent in by her GP with a threatened abortion. Her name was Wanda Firmin, and she and her husband had been trying for a baby for several years. She was in a highly emotional state, and Sarah attempted to calm her down.

'You just don't understand. We've waited years, and now this has to happen.'

'Please try and calm down, Mrs Firmin,' said Sarah. 'Nothing has happened yet and maybe nothing will, but getting upset won't help anything, you know. You must try and get some rest.'

'When am I going to see a proper doctor? I only saw that youngster when I came in—I want to see someone in charge.'

'Another doctor will be along to see you shortly,' said Sarah calmly.

Leaving the patient to rest, she made her way to the office, where she found Ria. 'Is Dr O'Neill coming up to see Mrs Firmin, Ria?'

Ria shook her head. 'No, he's off duty today.'

At her words Sarah felt a pang, then she shook herself. What difference should it make to her whether Liam was on duty or not? She was getting as bad as Tina.

'The registrar is coming to see her shortly,' continued Ria. 'Why? Is she getting agitated?'

'Yes. She says she wants to see a proper doctor, that she only saw a youngster when she came in.'

'We'd better not tell Philip that,' Ria grinned, then as Sarah was about to leave the office she said, 'Oh, Sarah, would you remove Mrs Baines's suture, please?'

Sarah returned to the ward, told Mrs Firmin that the registrar was coming to see her, then prepared a dressing trolley which she wheeled down the ward to Mrs Baines's bed, which was almost hidden behind a mass of flowers and 'Get Well' cards.

Mrs Baines lowered the brightly covered paperback she had been reading. 'That looks ominous,' she said, eyeing the trolley. 'Is it for me?'

Sarah nodded. 'I'm afraid it is.'

'So what delights have you got lined up for this morning? Oh, no, don't tell me. I've been dreading

this; it's my stitches, isn't it?' Mrs Baines took off
her glasses and put down her book, while Sarah drew
the curtains round her bed.

'It is, although it isn't stitches — there is in fact only
one stitch,' said Sarah as she cut open a paper pack,
shook out a pair of surgical gloves and pulled them
on.

'Only one stitch?' Mrs Baines stared up at her in
amazement. 'I though there'd be at least ten.'

Sarah smiled and shook her head. 'No, it isn't
done like that these days. You have one long stitch,
a bit like a blanket stitch holding everything together.
Now, let's just ease this dressing pad off. . . There;
believe it or not, but that's the worst bit over. Now
let's have a look. Oh, yes, that's a nice neat wound.'
She picked up a spray from the trolley. 'Now, this
will be a bit cold,' she said, spraying the wound.
Then, cutting the black suture with a pair of stitch-
cutters, she told Mrs Baines to take a deep breath,
then gently but firmly she pulled the long suture free
of the wound. 'There, that's done,' she said.

'Is that all?' Mrs Baines looked surprised.

'Yes. I'll just cover the wound with a dry dressing
pad in case there's any slight oozing.'

'So all that worrying was for nothing? I honestly
didn't feel a thing.' Mrs Baines sighed. 'I can't wait
to get home now, Nurse. Don't get me wrong, you've
all been very kind, but. . .'

'I know; there's no place like your own home, is
there?'

'Nurse, when the surgeon came round to see me
yesterday, he said something about some therapy.

What do you think he meant?' Mrs Baines looked anxious.

'He probably meant Hormone Replacement Therapy,' said Sarah. 'Because you've lost your ovaries as well as your womb your body will stop producing oestrogen, so the therapy will replace that. It will help with any unpleasant symptoms of the menopause, and it's also believed that it prevents osteoporosis or thinning of the bones. But you must remember you've had major surgery and you'll have to take things very quietly for a time,' Sarah added as she began to clear up the empty dressing packs on the trolley.

Mrs Baines nodded. 'I know, so everyone keeps telling me — still, it shouldn't be too bad. My sister lives near by and my husband is very good.' She eased herself up on the bed and took a sip of orange squash from the tumbler on her locker. 'Are you married, Nurse?'

Sarah shook her head.

'Engaged?'

'No, but my boyfriend and I have been going together for a long time now.'

'Oh, you want to get that ring on your finger — that's what I keep telling my youngest daughter, but she just laughs at me and tells me that times have changed and that no one bothers with all that these days. Well, I think it's a shame. There's no romance any more.' Mrs Baines lowered her voice. 'I think men today just take everything for granted.' She sniffed, put on her glasses and picked up her paperback again, while Sarah took her trolley back down the ward, wondering if what Mrs Baines had said didn't have a grain of truth in it.

Before she went off duty she went through the list of new admissions for the following day.

When Ria saw what she was doing she said, 'Aren't you off duty tomorrow?'

Sarah nodded. 'I am, but I wanted to see what list I'd have waiting for me on Monday morning. It looks a pretty heavy one.'

'Yes, eight admissions. Some are only overnight stays—but the majority are for major surgery, so it'll be all go.'

'Mrs Baines and Mrs Woodmore will be going home, won't they?' asked Sarah.

'Well, Mrs Baines will,' Ria replied, glancing at her list, 'but I'm not sure about Mrs Woodmore.'

'Is there a problem?'

'Her temperature's up and I've sent a urine specimen to the lab.'

'That's a shame; she was looking forward to going home. I'll have a chat with her before I go. Don't worry,' Sarah added seeing Ria's expression change, 'I won't say anything about her temperature.'

She found Mrs Woodmore dozing and was about to move away and leave her to rest when the old lady opened her eyes.

'Hello, dear,' she said. 'Do you want to do something?'

'No, I just came to say goodbye; I'm going off duty now,' replied Sarah, noting Mrs Woodmore's flushed face.

'Will you be here tomorrow?'

'No, it's my day off.'

'Oh, I won't see you again, Nurse. I'm going home tomorrow. Thank you for all you've done for me. You've been very kind.'

'It's been a pleasure,' Sarah said gently then, leaning closer, she smoothed a wisp of white hair out of the old lady's eyes. 'I wish they were all like you.'

This seemed to please Mrs Woodmore, and when Sarah left she was smiling.

As Sarah walked out of the hospital to her car she felt the first few spots of rain. She pulled a face and looked up at the sky. A huge bank of angry slate-grey clouds were moving in from the west.

Moments later she was driving towards the sports complex and playing fields on the far side of town. By the time she'd parked the car and walked across two fields the rugby match had started.

She saw Gary immediately; his blond hair and stature stood out even in a field full of equally large rugby players. The rain had progressed to a steady drizzle, and miserably Sarah pulled up the hood of her waxed jacket. She knew from bitter experience that where this particular game was concerned rain would not stop play. Gary hadn't openly acknowledged her arrival, but, knowing him as she did, from the way he was playing she guessed he knew she was there.

She tried to ignore the rain and concentrate on the game, but found herself thinking about Helen's party that night. She was still apprehensive about Gary meeting Liam, but she wasn't sure why. Liam was nothing to her and most probably he would be taking another girl anyway. Sarah tried to dismiss the little pang she felt at the thought of seeing Liam with someone — after all, it really shouldn't matter to her what he did.

She hadn't told Gary about the party yet, and she wasn't sure what his reaction would be. Gary was very much a creature driven by his moods; if he was in a good mood he would probably think the party a brilliant idea, but if he wasn't she knew she could forget it.

The one thing guaranteed to put him in a good mood was winning, whether it was squash or a team game like rugby or soccer. Forcing her thoughts back to the game, Sarah began to shout the appropriate encouragement.

Her luck must have been in, for in spite of the fact that the weather did its utmost to be aggravating it was in triumphant mood that Gary's mud-caked team finally left the field.

'Hi, kid!' he shouted just before he disappeared to the club-room and the showers. 'I won't be long.'

His euphoria was still very much in evidence half an hour later when he collapsed in the passenger seat of her car. 'So how's my girl, then?' He leaned across and gave Sarah a brief kiss. He smelt of coal-tar soap.

'Wet,' she replied.

He stared at her in astonishment, as if getting wet should be of no consequence after such a victory. 'But did you see. . .did you see that last touchdown?'

'Yes, Gary, I saw. . .you were brilliant.' Her tone

softened as she saw the genuine excitement in his blue eyes. She glanced out of the window to where his team-mates were piling into an assortment of cars and vans. 'Where to now?' she asked, knowing full well what the answer would be.

'Celebration. . .what else?'

The pub was already crowded with rugby players and a few wives and girlfriends when they arrived. Someone had bought Gary a pint, and Sarah watched him drink it in one go, to noisy encouragement from his team-mates. He ordered another and a fruit juice for her, and she made her way to a table at the back of the pub, knowing that she wouldn't have Gary's attention for some while, not until the inquest on the match was over.

She was surprised when less than ten minutes later he joined her.

She smiled as he sat down. 'I didn't expect you yet. I thought you'd be involved in that for some time,' she nodded towards the bar, where noisy arguments were still in full swing.

'I wanted to talk to you,' he said, taking a mouthful of his drink, then setting his glass down on the table.

'That's nice.' She watched him, the shiny golden hair that fell across his forehead, the handsome, even features and the clear blue eyes which had been the first thing that had attracted her to him all those years ago. Then, spurred on by his obvious good humour, she said quickly, 'I wanted to talk to you as well. We've been invited to a party tonight.'

He threw her a quick glance, but she carried on, not giving him a chance to speak. 'You'll never guess—it's Helen Richards. You remember,' she said when a slight frown wrinkled his forehead, 'she used to go out with Chris.' He nodded then and she hurried on. 'Well, she's working at the hospital—in Theatre. She's having a party tonight to celebrate her and her boyfriend naming the day for their wedding, and she's asked us to go.'

'That would be fine,' said Gary, and for the first time she thought there was something odd in his manner. 'Except for one thing.'

'What's that? What is it, Gary—is there something wrong?'

'That's what I wanted to tell you. I won't be here.'

'What do you mean?' Sarah stared at him.

'You know I told you about the new depot Dad's opening in the Midlands? Well, the guy who was organising it has gone down with mumps. Dad's asked me to go up and take over for a couple of weeks. I'm sorry, Sarah, really I am—we don't seem to have seen very much of each other since you came back, do we?'

Slowly Sarah shook her head. 'No, Gary, we don't.' She sighed. 'I suppose it can't be helped. When are you going?'

'That's the crunch, I'm afraid. I have to go tonight.'

'Tonight? Whatever for?'

'Well, the depot's opening on Monday and there's still a hell of a lot to be done—I couldn't go this afternoon, of course, because of the match.'

'Of course.'

He glanced sharply at her. 'I say, I am sorry, kid. I'll make it up to you when I get back, honest, and

I'm really sorry about the party. Give my apologies to Helen, won't you?'

'I don't suppose I'll bother to go on my own,' she said flatly.

'Oh, you must—there'll be people there you know.' Gary stood up and looked down at her. 'By the way, is it Chris she's marrying? I haven't seen him for ages.'

'No, Gary, it isn't Chris. That relationship died years ago,' she said as she followed him from the pub.

After dropping Gary off at his home Sarah drove slowly back to Linfield House. Suddenly she felt miserable and depressed. She knew it wasn't Gary's fault that he had to go to the Midlands—it was his job, after all—but it seemed that ever since she'd come home to live she'd seen less and less of him. She knew her shift work would prove a problem to their social life, and of course the other big obstacle to their being together was his sporting activities. Now it seemed his job was being added to the list of difficulties.

It had stopped raining, the clouds had scattered and the darkening sky over the sea was tinged with crimson, promising a fine day to come. The esplanade was deserted except for one lone man walking his dog.

Sarah brought the car to a halt outside Linfield House and sat for a moment staring up at the pebble-dashed façade with its fresh yellow paintwork. Even her parents would have gone by now. She glanced at her watch; they would be well on the way of the first stage of their journey. With a sigh she climbed out of her car and shut the door. She had been so looking forward to her first weekend off duty; now the time loomed depressingly ahead.

As she let herself in to the house she heard the faint sounds of a popular TV quiz show coming from one of the ground-floor flats, but apart from that the house was in silence. Wearily she climbed the stairs, deciding the best thing she could do would be to run herself a hot bath, then eat her supper in front of the television. She would phone Helen the next day and apologise about missing the party. There was no way she wanted to go now — without Gary.

When she reached her landing she fumbled in her bag for her key, then she heard a sound behind her. She turned sharply. A strip of light was showing beneath the door of the empty flat.

She froze. Someone was in there.

Then she remembered her mother saying that her father had said someone had enquired about the flat. Had someone moved in? Or was it an intruder?

She stepped nearer to the door and listened, but there was no further sound from inside. The silence was unnerving, and Sarah felt a sickening wave of panic.

Then suddenly she knew she had to pull herself together and confront whoever was in the flat. Straightening her shoulders, she raised her hand to knock, but before her knuckles touched the door it was suddenly pulled open.

Sarah gasped and blinked in the surge of light, then stared in astonishment.

Liam O'Neill stood in the open doorway.

CHAPTER SIX

'YOU!' She stared at him in bewilderment. 'What in the world are you doing here?'

'Hello, Sarah. I was waiting for you to come in.'

'But. . . I don't understand. . . How did you get in here?' She tried to look past him into the flat.

'I have a key.'

Slowly the truth began to dawn. 'You don't mean it's you who's rented this flat?' she said in disbelief.

'I'm afraid it is. I'm your new neighbour.'

She frowned, suddenly aware that her heart, which had almost turned over when she had seen him, was now thumping very fast.

'How did you know about the flat?' Her words came out almost like an accusation.

'I saw an advertisement on the noticeboard in the canteen.'

She continued to stare at him, her brain unwilling to accept what he was saying.

'Look, come in and I'll explain.' He stood aside for her to enter the flat.

She hesitated for a moment, then walked past him and stood in the centre of the sitting-room, while he closed the door and followed her.

'It really was the most incredible coincidence,' he said. 'I'd been looking for other accommodation for some time. I was really fed up with the flat I had at the hospital; it was cramped and very noisy. Then I saw the advertisement and came here to look at this flat.'

'Did you know I lived here?' queried Sarah.

'How could I? There was no name on the advert, only the address. I didn't associate the name until this morning when I moved my gear over here and paid my first month's rent. When I saw the name Bartrum on the receipt I mentioned you, and my new landlord turned out to be your father. When I explained who I was he seemed relieved that some-one you knew would be renting the flat, especially as it's next to yours.'

Still Sarah stared at him. His explanation sounded reasonable. . .and yet. . . She shook her head.

'What's wrong?' he asked gently. 'Don't you like the idea of having me for a neighbour? I'm quite harmless, I promise.'

She looked up into his face then, and the look of amusement in his eyes had been replaced by one of innocence. She hesitated for only one more moment, then she smiled, and he seemed to visibly relax.

Helplessly she looked around the flat, which was very similar to her own. 'Do you have everything you need? I'm afraid my parents have gone away on holiday. . .'

'Yes,' he said quickly, 'your father said they were going—Thailand, isn't it?' He glanced round as he spoke at the simple but comfortable furnishings. 'This is great. You should have seen what I had to make do with before. How many other tenants are there in the house?'

'Three,' she answered. 'There are six flats altogether — my parents', mine, this one and three others.'

'It's a lovely house.'

She nodded wistfully. 'It was when we ran it as a guest-house. I think it's been spoilt now. . . Well, Liam —— ' she gave a little shrug ' — what else can I say? Welcome to Linfield House.'

'Thanks.' He smiled, and that wicked glint of amusement was back.

Hurriedly Sarah looked away. 'Well, if you have everything you need, I'll leave you to it. . .'

'Oh, don't run away. Stay and have a cup of tea or something.'

'No, no — really. I've been out all day. I have things to do.' She moved towards the door.

Liam glanced at his watch. 'You mean getting ready for Helen's party?'

She paused with one hand on the door-handle. She'd forgotten all about Helen's party.

'How are you getting there?' he asked.

'Actually, Liam, I've decided not to go to the party.'

'And why is that?' His voice was soft now, the Irish lilt more pronounced.

She hesitated again; the silence lengthened and it was Liam who broke it. 'Yesterday I could have sworn you were looking forward to the party, so what's happened today to make you change your mind?'

She took a deep breath. She might as well tell him the real reason as attempt to lie — something she was always hopeless at. 'Helen invited both Gary and myself to the party. . .'

'Yes?' He waited for her to go on.

'Well, Gary's been called away unexpectedly.'

Silence greeted her words, and when she half turned and looked at Liam he looked as if he was still waiting for her explanation.

She shrugged and made to turn back to the door and make her escape.

'Is that it? Is that the reason you're not going?' There was surprise in his tone.

She nodded. 'Yes, I suppose it is.'

'But why? I don't understand.'

'I just decided I didn't want to go without him, that's all.'

'Ah, is he the jealous type? Would he object to your going on your own?'

'Of course not. Don't be silly; I went to hundreds of parties when I was in training, and I'm sure Gary did the same—in fact, he told me to go and enjoy myself.'

'So why aren't you?'

'I don't know.' Sarah's voice rose slightly. 'I suppose I just didn't like the idea of going on my own.' As soon as she'd said it, she knew it was a mistake.

'Well, if that's the only reason, it's easily solved,' he said, and his voice was soft again. 'I too was going on my own, so the simple solution is that we go together.'

'I. . .I'm not sure that's a very good idea, Liam. . .'

'Nonsense, it's a terrific idea; after all, you've

already said your boyfriend doesn't mind you going. Go and get yourself ready, and we'll go in my car. Nine o'clock be all right?'

With her head spinning Sarah finally let herself into her flat. The first thing she saw was a white envelope that had been slipped under her door.

It was a note from her parents saying how pleased they were that they had been able to let the empty flat to a colleague of hers, and that they could now go happily off on holiday knowing she was all right. With a wry grimace she crumpled the note and dropped it into her waste-bin, wondering what her father would say if he knew just how much interest Liam O'Neill had shown towards her since she had met him. Her parents had obviously been so relieved to let the flat to a doctor, and to someone who actually was acquainted with her, when there were so many undesirable characters around, that no other possibility would have crossed their minds. And why should it? she thought as she ran herself a bath. As far as they were concerned she was perfectly happy in her relationship with Gary.

And she was, wasn't she? Perfectly happy with Gary? She frowned, unzipped her jeans and pulled off her sweater. Of course she was, she reassured herself as moments later she stepped into the scented foaming bath. She'd simply been upset and miserable that he'd had to go away, and she'd been taken unawares by Liam.

She frowned and lay back in the soft bubbles. It had been a shock to find Liam in the flat—she couldn't deny that—and at first she'd felt a sense of annoyance that somehow he had contrived the whole thing, but then, when he'd explained, it really did look as if it had all been a coincidence. She wasn't yet sure how she felt about the fact that Liam would actually be living in the same building as her — but why should it matter?

She sighed and, raising her arms, secured her long hair on the top of her head, tying it with a piece of ribbon. Deep down she knew the answers to these questions, just as she knew the reason for the sense of unease that had hovered at the back of her mind since she'd first set eyes on the handsome Irish doctor. For just as Liam had made it plain that he found her attractive, she knew that he had triggered some similar desire inside her.

She was also well aware that she had to ignore these emotions. She had Gary, theirs was a long-standing relationship and she didn't want to hurt him, and if that wasn't enough she was also aware of Liam O'Neill's reputation as a heartbreaker.

He had talked her into going to the party with him, and it was quite true — Gary had told her to go and to enjoy herself. Maybe there wouldn't be any harm in it after all, she thought as some time later, wrapped in a large fluffy bath towel, she stood in front of her wardrobe and tried to decide what she should wear. She would of course have to make quite certain that Liam knew the score and that there were to be no strings attached, but once that was out of the way there was no reason why they shouldn't have a good time.

Finally she decided to wear a short red skirt and a

tiny fitted black jacket over a red camisole top. Her dark hair she teased into a casual tousled cloud and she applied a little more make-up than she wore for work, accentuating her almond-shaped eyes and her high cheekbones. After a light spray of her favourite musky perfume she was ready, and as she came out of her bedroom she heard the click of Liam's door.

His car was a vintage MG sports model. In black and shining chrome with a soft top, it was quite obviously his pride and joy. He opened the passenger door for her with a flourish then took his place beside her.

Sarah stole a glance in his direction, quite clearly in the light from an overhead streetlamp seeing the frown on his face as he fitted the key into the ignition. He was dressed in a casual bottle-green sweatshirt and modern, dark-coloured trousers in a loose-fitting style. He looked very handsome, and Sarah felt her pulse race as she recalled the look in his eyes when he had come out of his room on to the landing and caught sight of her. She had panicked slightly and, not giving him a chance to comment, had hurried down the stairs ahead of him.

The rain of earlier had quite cleared, giving way to a quiet, clear autumn night with just a hint of a chill in the air that maybe heralded a dawn frost.

They drew away from Linfield House and drove slowly along the esplanade. One or two late-season tourists were taking an evening stroll, heading for the only bar that remained open. As they passed the bright, neon-lighted entrance Sarah glanced back and said, 'I was going to offer to drive my car so that you could have a drink.'

He smiled. 'There's no need for that.'

'I wouldn't have minded. I'm quite used to it.'

'What do you mean?' Liam queried.

'I drive Gary everywhere — for that reason. He got breathalysed once. He was just under the limit, but it shook him, and his father warned him that if it happened again he would be out of a job.'

'Well, there's no fear of that with me,' Liam told her, then added casually, 'I don't drink.'

Sarah stared at him in surprise.

'Go on, say it — everyone else does,' he laughed, and changed gear. 'You've never before met an Irishman who didn't drink.'

'Have you never drunk?' she asked.

'Oh, yes, I was weaned on the stuff and I drank my way through medical school with the best of them. . . That was the problem.'

'Oh, I see. . .'

He laughed again. 'Don't get me wrong, I'm not an alcoholic, but if I'd carried on the way I was it could have become a problem, if not to my job, then to my liver.'

'So what happened?' She was curious but also slightly relieved. There had until now been something about Liam that had suggested that he was too good to be true. What he had just told her implied that he was as human as anyone.

'Chloe came into my life and it was either her or drink. There was no contest — she won.'

'Chloe. . .?.' she asked faintly, wondering suddenly whether there had been something obvious she had missed, like a girlfriend or even a fiancée she hadn't heard about.

'Yes. She's beautiful, isn't she?' Lovingly he patted the dashboard of the MG, and Sarah drew in her breath to suppress a chuckle as she realised what he meant.

After a moment he went on to explain further. 'The drink-driving laws over quantity are so ambiguous that I decided there was only one thing for it. If I wanted to drive Chloe without any restrictions, I'd have to give up the hard stuff completely.'

'And you did? Just like that?'

He nodded. 'Yep, haven't touched a drop since.'

Sarah fell silent, thinking how Gary would have found that option impossible.

'So where's he gone?' asked Liam suddenly, and she started. It was almost as if he had been able to read her thoughts.

'I'm sorry?'

'Your boyfriend. You said he'd been called away.' Deftly, with his eyes on the road, Liam negotiated the roundabout at the approach to the town.

'That's right, he has. His father's company is opening a new branch in the Midlands. Apparently the man who was setting it up has gone sick, so Mr Jones asked Gary to go.'

'Has he always worked for his father?' asked Liam.

She nodded. 'Yes, he went into the company straight from school.'

'So he didn't go away to university?'

She shook her head. 'He flunked his A levels — he

spent all his time playing sport when he should have been studying. But then I suppose it didn't really matter. He didn't need to go to university. It had always been accepted that he'd go into the family firm.'

'Does he still live at home?' There was an incredulous note in Liam's voice.

'Yes. But I suppose you can't really blame him,' Sarah said, rushing to Gary's defence. 'He has his mother doing everything for him.'

'I think everyone should get away, leave the nest and broaden their horizons. . .' He turned slightly towards her.

'I agree with you. It did me no end of good learning to be independent,' she said.

'And now you've come back,' he said softly.

She threw him a sharp glance. 'Are you implying that it's a mistake?'

He shrugged. 'Only you can answer that. I personally think you can only go forward, that we progress and outgrow situations, but you may feel differently. You may feel everything is as good as it ever was. . .or maybe even better. . .'

Sarah bit her lip and looked out of the car at the lighted shop windows. In a way Liam's words were echoing Helen's when she had implied that she and Chris had outgrown each other. Was it as good as it had ever been with Gary, or had she been clinging to a dream?

As her thoughts turned to Gary again she felt a renewed twinge of guilt. There he was, travelling through the night in order to work, while she was

sitting beside this very attractive Irish doctor in his
sports car on her way to a party.

But Gary had told her to go, she reminded herself,
only to have a small, still voice immediately answer
back that when he'd told her that he hadn't been
quite aware what the situation would be.

She swallowed, then, taking a deep breath, she
said, 'Liam, talking of Gary——'

'Were we?' he interrupted, briefly taking his eyes
from the road. 'I thought we were talking about you.'

'Yes, well,' she went on hurriedly, 'we were talking
about him before, and I think we need to get
something absolutely straight.'

'We do?' His tone was innocent now.

'Yes, I want you to understand that even though
I've agreed to come to this party with you that's to
be all there is in it.'

'But of course.' He sounded hurt. 'Are you sug-
gesting I had an ulterior motive?'

'Well. . . I. . .'

'Oh, come on, Sarah, if a guy can't ask a girl to
come to a harmless staff party with him without her
assuming he has an ulterior motive, then I think it's
a pretty poor show. Look, relax—I promise I won't
molest you or anything. Let's just enjoy the evening.'

Suddenly Sarah felt extremely foolish. Had she
been reading more into his intentions than was
warranted? And had she now led him to believe just
that? Would he now think that she had jumped to
the automatic conclusion that he was interested in
her?

In an attempt to cover her confusion, she tried to

change the subject. 'Have you been to the hospital today?' she asked as they sped past the large, familiar lighted building.

'No—I haven't had the time. You don't realise how many possessions you've accumulated until you come to move them. Have you been in today?'

'Yes, I did an early, half-day shift.'

'How were things?'

'Mrs Baines was getting excited about going home.'

'And Ellie Woodmore, I suppose?' queried Liam.

'Well. . .' she began.

'Is there a problem?' he asked quickly, and she immediately detected the concern in his voice.

'According to Ria she had a raised temperature, and when I went in to see her I noticed she looked flushed,' she told him.

'Poor Ellie; I hope there won't be complications there. She's done so well up until now, especially as she has a history of chronic bronchitis. What else was going on?' He'd slowed the car now as he searched for Helen's house.

'Well, there are eight admissions tomorrow. Are you on duty?' asked Sarah.

He shook his head as he brought the car to a halt. 'No, it's my long weekend off. I thought I'd better get some training in for the walk. How about you? Are you on duty?'

'No, but I'd reckoned on a blissful lie-in,' she replied, then as a motorbike roared up and stopped in front of them she added, 'Oh, here's Philip.' Then, remembering what had happened that morning, she said, 'He admitted a patient today with a threatened abortion. She called him a youngster, and asked me when she was going to see a proper doctor.'

Liam laughed. 'I'm not surprised, with that baby face of his.' Then, growing serious again, he asked, 'What happened with the patient?'

'She's under observation and on bed rest. She's thirty-four, in week twelve of her pregnancy, and it's her first baby. She was about to go for ultrasound when I left.'

Liam nodded, and as they got out of the car Sarah marvelled at how involved he was with everything that happened on his ward, even when he was off duty.

Liam had been quite right when he had said that he'd thought Helen was going to try and cram half the staff of the hospital into her tiny house, for when she opened the front door to them and to Philip, who had joined them outside, it appeared as if the house was bursting with bodies and vibrating to the sound of Madonna. Light spilled out from the hallway into the small front garden.

'Sarah!' cried Helen. 'You came! I am glad, and you've brought Ga. . .' She trailed off as she caught sight of first Liam, then Philip.

'Gary couldn't come, Helen; he sends his apologies,' Sarah said quickly. 'Liam gave me a lift and we met Philip outside.'

'Oh, good.' Helen looked a bit perplexed for a moment, then she seemed to catch Liam's eye and she grinned. 'Well, come on in—if you can get in, that is. Food's through there——' she pointed to what appeared to be a conservatory at the back of the house '—booze is in the kitchen—oh, and music in the lounge.'

Already people were sitting on the stairs, and as they passed the lounge Sarah noticed it was in semi-darkness, while a few couples danced to the throbbing beat.

She caught a glimpse of Lucy in the kitchen with a tall, ginger-haired man whom she guessed to be her husband, Colin, then Liam was asking her what she wanted to drink.

While he attempted to make his way through the throng around the kitchen, Sarah leaned against a bookcase in the hall and looked round to see if she could see anyone else she recognised. Feeling someone's eyes on her, she glanced upwards and saw a girl sitting on the top stair. She was dressed in a tight-fitting black dress with her short dark hair gelled into a spiky style so that it appeared wet. For a moment Sarah didn't recognise her, then as she stood up she realised it was Tina. She smiled, opened her mouth to say hello, but before she had time to utter a sound Tina had turned on her heel and disappeared into one of the bedrooms.

CHAPTER SEVEN

As with most parties the most stimulating conversation seemed to be taking place in the kitchen. When Liam returned with Sarah's drink Lucy suddenly spotted them and they were drawn quickly into her group. She introduced Sarah to her husband Colin, then while the two men were discussing Colin's job in the building trade she turned back to Sarah, an amused but interested expression on her face.

Sarah, anticipating what was coming, clutched her glass and tried to adopt a nonchalant expression.

'So how do you come to be with him?' murmured Lucy, subtly tilting her head in Liam's direction.

'It's a long story,' Sarah murmured back.

'Tell me; we have all night. I'm fascinated.'

Sarah threw a quick glance in Liam's direction, but he seemed to be in deep conversation with Colin and unaware of the rest of the babble that was going on around him.

'It's not what you think,' she said.

'And how do you know what I'm thinking?' There was a mischievous gleam in Lucy's eyes as she contemplated Sarah over the rim of her wine glass.

Sarah gave an exasperated sigh. 'You're thinking that Liam and I have come here as a couple.'

'And you haven't?' Lucy's eyes widened.

94

'Of course not. Liam only brought me here because I'd said I wasn't coming.'

'And why did you say you weren't coming? You were looking forward to it earlier.'

'I know, but that was when I thought Gary was coming with me.'

'Ah, Gary, yes, I'd forgotten about him,' said Lucy. 'So where is he?'

Sarah glanced at her watch. 'At this moment I should imagine he's hurtling towards Birmingham.'

'Birmingham? Whatever's he going there for?'

'He's been sent up there by his father — it's to do with his job,' explained Sarah, moving back into a corner as she spoke, to help make space for another group of people who had piled into the kitchen.

'So it was a case of exit Gary and enter Liam?' Lucy grinned.

'You make it sound dreadful,' protested Sarah half laughingly. 'It's not like that at all. It was simply that Liam thought I wouldn't come to the party if I didn't have someone to go with, so he persuaded me to come with him.'

'So when did all this happen? You weren't on duty this afternoon, were you?'

Sarah shook her head, and suddenly she couldn't bring herself to explain about Liam and the flat at Linfield House. There was no telling what Lucy would read into that, in her present mischief-making frame of mind.

'No, I wasn't on duty,' she said, then added vaguely, 'I saw him. . .around. . .' She trailed off, hoping Lucy would leave it at that. Out of the corner of her eye she saw that Liam was heading for the lounge with Helen, presumably to dance.

'I should think this would just about make Tina's night,' said Lucy cryptically. 'Does she know you're here?'

Sarah nodded. 'Yes, she saw us arrive.'

'Oh, God. And I have to work with her tomorrow. She's been throwing out hints all week to try to make sure that Liam would be here tonight, and now he's turned up with you!' Lucy chuckled wickedly and turned to pass her empty glass to her husband for refilling.

Suddenly Sarah felt sorry for Tina. 'I think perhaps I'll have a chat with her,' she said to Lucy. 'You know, put her straight on a few points, tell her there's nothing going on between me and Liam.'

Lucy laughed. 'Well, you can try, but I don't envy you. Tina's not the easiest girl in the world to reason with—in fact, if I were you, I wouldn't bother; it's not as if she has any claim on Liam, after all.'

'Even so, I wouldn't want to ruin her evening.' As she spoke Sarah turned to see if she could see Tina, and almost collided with a tall, dark-haired man who was carrying two full glasses of beer. 'Oh, I'm sorry. . .'

'Oh, Sarah,' Lucy intervened, 'this is Alan, Helen's fiancé.'

'Hello, Alan,' she smiled, taking an instant liking to him as his face lit up.

'Sarah! Well, hello. Helen's been telling me a lot about you.'

'Oh, dear, that sounds ominous,' she laughed.

'We'll have a chat later. . .' he said, trying to hold

the drinks out of harm's way as he was jostled towards the door.

When she turned back to Lucy it was to find that she and Colin had been drawn into another conversation. She glanced round to see if there was anyone else in the kitchen whom she knew, and saw Philip standing alone in the corner.

He looked uneasy, as if he didn't really like parties. Sarah edged her way through the crush of people to talk to him.

'Do you know all these people?' she gasped when she finally reached his side.

'Some of them, but not everyone. I haven't been at the hospital that long.'

'I should think everyone's been there longer than me. I hardly know anyone,' said Sarah, gazing round at the unfamiliar faces.

'Would. . .would you like to dance?' stammered Philip. He said it as if he expected her to refuse, as if he was used to refusals.

'Thank you, Philip, I should love to,' she replied, smiling at his surprised expression. She set her glass down on the draining-board, wondering if it would still be there when she came back.

They fought their way through to the dimly lit lounge, and as she danced with Philip her eyes gradually became accustomed to the dark and she realised that Liam and Helen were still dancing. Then the beat slowed and Philip drew her awkwardly towards him. They swayed to the new smoochy rhythm, then over Philip's shoulder she caught sight of Liam. He in turn was watching her over Helen's shoulder.

She smiled, expecting his usual smile in response, but his expression was serious, almost intense. They were so close that if she'd reached out her hand she could have touched him. Still his expression didn't change as he continued to gaze at her, then just as she was thinking that neither of them was going to be able to look away, when it felt as if their glances were locked for all time, Philip moved her round so that Liam was obscured from her vision.

It was only then that she realised how tense she had become, and she was forced to make a conscious effort to relax. When she was able to look again she realised that Liam and Helen had gone, and later, when she and Philip wandered back to the kitchen, she found them deep in conversation.

As she approached they looked up, and when they saw her they stopped what they were saying almost as if they'd been talking about her.

'Enjoying yourself?' asked Liam, and there was no trace of the intense look that had been in those dark eyes earlier. When she nodded he glanced at Philip. 'You want to watch him—these junior housemen simply aren't to be trusted.'

Sarah and Helen laughed, and Philip flushed to the roots of his blond hair.

'I'd trust Philip with my life,' said Sarah in an attempt to cover his embarrassment, 'and just to prove I mean what I say I'm going to have supper with him. Are you coming, Philip?'

They filled their plates from the delicious buffet

that Helen had prepared and perched themselves on the stairs to eat, and it wasn't until much later, when Sarah had gone upstairs to a bedroom to freshen up, that she found an opportunity to speak to Tina.

The girl was standing in front of the dressing-table mirror applying fresh lipstick. She glanced at Sarah's reflection in the mirror as she came into the room, but she didn't turn round.

'It's a good party, isn't it?' said Sarah, wondering how she could get round to what she wanted to say.

Tina raised her shoulders slightly in a gesture which implied that the party was all right but that it wasn't anything special.

'I'm glad I came,' Sarah struggled on valiantly. 'I'd decided not to, you know.'

Tina's eyes met hers in the mirror and her expression clearly asked if that was the case why had she bothered to come.

'It was my boyfriend, you see,' Sarah went on.

'Your boyfriend?' Tina stood very still, her lipstick poised in one hand, then she frowned, clearly puzzled.

'Yes. He was supposed to come with me, but he got called away at the last moment. If Liam hadn't offered to give me a lift I wouldn't have bothered to come. Anyway, I'm glad I did, because I'd promised Helen I'd be here.'

By the time Sarah had finished speaking, Tina had stepped back, making room for her at the mirror. Before she took her place Sarah shot a glance at the other girl to try and see whether her explanation had had the desired effect. It was, however, difficult to tell, because Tina was one of those girls who seemed to have a permanently sulky expression.

Sarah sighed as she watched her leave the bed-room. Well, she'd done her best to make her realise that there was nothing between herself and Liam O'Neill. Whether she'd succeeded and the girl had believed her remained to be seen, but at least she'd tried.

When she returned downstairs she was claimed, first by Colin, and then by Alan, to dance. Her first impression concerning Alan proved to be correct— he really was very nice, and just the right type for Helen.

As they danced Sarah found herself envying her friend that her future seemed secure.

'So when's the big day to be?' she asked Alan.

'Easter Saturday,' he replied.

'Oh, how lovely. There's something romantic about an Easter bride, and Helen will certainly make a lovely bride.'

He smiled. 'I agree, but then I'm prejudiced. How about you? Helen tells me you've been going steady for a long time now—no big day arranged yet?'

'Oh, no, nothing like that. We've hardly even discussed it.'

Alan shook his head. 'I'll have to tell that guy of yours to buck up his ideas, otherwise he'll be losing you.'

They danced a little longer, and Sarah reflected that it really was true—she and Gary had never seriously discussed settling down together.

As she followed Alan from the lounge he headed

for the kitchen, and she stood in the hall for a moment wondering where Lucy was, then suddenly, taking her completely by surprise, she felt someone's arm go round her.

'Don't you think it's high time you had a dance with me? After all, if it weren't for me you wouldn't even be here.'

She didn't have to turn round, she knew who it was, but she had been unable to prevent her heart skipping a beat at the unexpected feel of his arm around her. In an attempt to lighten the mood she said, 'I thought you'd never ask.'

In the semi-darkness of the lounge they began to move to the pulsating beat of the number that had topped the charts for three weeks running. The excitement caught Sarah, quickening her pulse, heightening her awareness of the other figures in the room—mere outlines in the darkness who moved to the frantic pace—of the smell—a heady blend of perfumes and colognes and of bodies, male and female, and cigarette smoke—but most of all of the man in front of her.

He was simply a silhouette, the light from the hall only catching his dark hair or his features when someone opened the door, but he moved with an almost feline grace until, unexpectedly, the music stopped.

Couples around them moved towards the door laughing and gasping, in search of refreshment, and the tempo changed to a soft sensual rhythm.

Without a moment's hesitation Liam drew her into

his arms. With a sigh Sarah leaned against him, aware only of how right it felt.

Then as they slowly began to sway to the music she moved her arms, linking her hands at the back of his neck. He lowered his head so that his cheek was resting against hers, and she felt the slight roughness, the beginnings of stubble, caught the musky male aroma of him, and later, when dreamily she shifted position, was aware of his arousal, of the effect she was having on him.

She knew she should move, should suggest they go back to the others. She knew it was dangerous being like this with this man, knew it was playing with fire, but somehow she was incapable of doing anything. It was as if they moved in a dream, as if their movements were totally beyond their control.

Then finally, when it seemed as if they would go on forever simply holding each other and gently swaying in time to the heart-rending lyrics of the music, Liam straightened up, his hands moving down her back, briefly encircling her waist.

She gazed up at him, mesmerised by his dark eyes, then he brought his hands up to briefly cup her face and she felt a thrill course through her body.

For a moment that seemed suspended in time he looked down at her, before giving a deep sigh. Then it was over, and he was leading her back into the bright, harsh reality of the hall and the hubbub in the kitchen beyond.

'Here's Sarah now.' Alan touched Helen's arm as Sarah stood in the doorway blinking in the light.

Helen turned sharply. 'Oh, good. Sarah, did you

bring the tickets. . .?' Her voice trailed away in confusion as she caught sight of Sarah's flushed face, then she looked quickly beyond her to Liam.

It was Liam who smoothly took over. 'Yes, Sarah, have you got the barbecue tickets with you?'

But Sarah had clapped her hand over her mouth. 'Oh, I forgot!' she said.

'You mean you've missed a perfect opportunity like this?' Alan laughed. 'You'll have to get your recruits better trained than that, Liam.'

Liam laughed too. 'Yes, I can see some training is in order.'

They all looked towards Sarah as if they expected some explanation for her forgetfulness. She swallowed and turned away. How could she tell them that finding that Liam had moved into Linfield House had put everything out of her mind, including the tickets that she had planned to sell at the party?

Out of the corner of her eye she saw Philip come out of the lounge with Tina and realised they must have been in there while she had been dancing with Liam. Quickly she looked down, for now there was no way she could look Tina in the eye.

Suddenly she wanted to go. Too many things had happened that day and her emotions seemed to be in a jangled heap. Almost as if he anticipated her change of mood, Liam touched her arm.

'Ready to go?' he murmured.

She nodded, they made their goodbyes, and, conscious of Lucy's speculative look, escaped outside.

As they drove home Sarah remained quiet, only

too aware that Liam had been as affected as she by
their closeness while they had danced.

But had he? She stole a glance at his profile. She
had already accused him of ulterior motives, which
he had denied, making her feel foolish. Was his
behaviour typical of him? Did he act like that with
anyone he danced with? Or had it been special? And
if it had, what then? Would he try to recapture the
mood when they got back to Linfield House? And if
he did, what would she do? Desperately she tried to
pull herself together. She mustn't encourage him,
whatever happened, for she had a strong feeling that
it wouldn't take too much encouragement for Liam
O'Neill to take the situation further.

She wasn't free—she'd made that quite plain to
him, or at least, she thought she had. Maybe he
would need reminding of that fact when they got
home. Suddenly all she wanted was to get it over
with so that she could go to bed.

Because she'd become so lost in her thoughts she
jumped when Liam suddenly spoke. 'Would you
mind very much if we called into the hospital before
we go home?'

'What, at this time of night?' The clock on the
dashboard said it was five minutes to two.

'We should just about be in time for coffee.' He
grinned, then grew serious again. 'I want to see how
Ellie is.'

Five minutes later they parked the MG in a
consultant's space in front of the main entrance and
entered the building.

The hospital at night was a strange, eerie place of

silent, dimly lit corridors bearing little resemblance to the teeming hustle and bustle that took place there every day. Liam had a word with the night porter on duty, then they took the lift up to the gynae wards.

When they stepped out of the lift and walked past the sluice they caught the sudden sweet fragrance of the patients' flowers which had been massed there overnight, and as they approached the office an auxiliary passed them wheeling a commode to the post-op ward.

Sarah didn't know the senior staff nurse who was on duty, but Liam introduced her to Sarah as Alison May. 'We've been to Helen Richards's party,' he went on to explain.

'Some people get all the luck,' grumbled Alison. 'My social life is practically non-existent since I've been on nights. I suppose you've come in here for coffee?'

'Something like that.' Liam gave his most persuasive smile. 'But first I wanted to check what's happening with Ellie Woodmore. I understand she had a temperature this morning.'

Alison nodded and, turning to the desk, she went rapidly through the pile of patient records. 'Yes, I'm afraid she's developed a urinary tract infection.' She handed him a folder. 'She's on Trimethoprim. Actually she's awake if you want to see her — I've just taken her a cup of tea.'

'All right.' Liam scanned her notes, then closed the folder. 'I'll just take a quick look at her. I won't be long,' he said to Sarah as he left the office.

'Mrs Woodmore was looking forward to going

home tomorrow,' said Sarah as Liam pulled the door to behind him.

'Well, that's out of the question now,' said Alison, then she said curiously, 'You say you've been to Helen Richards's party?'

'Yes.' Sarah turned and saw a look on Alison's face that she'd come to recognise only too well in the last few days. She sighed. 'And before you ask — no, I'm not going out with Dr O'Neill. He simply gave me a lift, that's all.'

Alison grinned, walked across the office to the coffee-machine and took three mugs off a shelf. 'Sorry, it's just that where he's concerned speculation is rife. I suppose it's because he's so dishy — let's face it, when was the last time you saw a SHO like that?'

Sarah was forced to laugh. 'Yes, I suppose you're right; he is very nice,' she admitted as she watched Alison pour the coffee, then as the other girl handed her one of the mugs she said, 'By the way, how's Wanda Firmin?'

'She's OK; she's still resting. The ultrasound was normal and it looks as if things have settled down.'

'I'm so glad. She really wants this baby.' Sarah sipped the hot coffee and looked up as Liam came back into the room. 'How's Ellie?'

'Very calm. She's already worked out that she won't be going home in the morning.'

'Is she too disappointed?' asked Sarah as Alison handed Liam his mug of coffee and he perched on the edge of the desk to drink it.

He shook his head. 'No, she seems to take everything in her stride. Who's the new admission, Alison?'

'Sharon Jesson—emergency referral by her GP. Presented with low abdominal pain. Last menstrual period was six weeks ago.'

'Ectopic pregnancy?' asked Liam.

'Sounds like it. She's waiting to go to Theatre now. Her husband is with her.'

'Who's on call?'

'Mr Chang.'

Liam nodded. 'Busy week coming up, I hear.'

'Yes, eight admissions tomorrow.' Alison pulled a face, then, glancing at her watch, said, 'I hope you two aren't on an early shift?'

'No, we're both off duty.' Liam drained his mug and stood up. 'But we should be going anyway. Thanks for the coffee. Ready, Sarah?'

They were mostly silent on the drive back to the sea-front. The night was still and bright, but the chill in the air had grown sharper.

'The sea looks calm,' observed Liam as they stepped out of the car.

'You should see it sometimes in October,' remarked Sarah, 'when there's a south-westerly blowing in.'

'I should imagine it gets quite terrifying.' They had stopped and were staring out to sea.

'I suppose it could be. But I love it when it's like that, when it's wild and the waves crash right across the road.'

'Well, I hope it isn't like that the night of our

barbecue,' said Liam as they turned and walked up the steps to the front door.

'What will you do if it is?' asked Sarah curiously.

'We'll just have to have some sort of party in the social club, but it wouldn't be the same.'

They were halfway up the stairs by then, and Sarah turned. 'Liam, I'm sorry I forgot the tickets,' she said.

'That's OK. There's plenty of time to get rid of them yet.'

'Even so. . .' they paused as they reached their landing '. . .it would have been a perfect opportunity to have sold some.'

'Never mind.' He smiled and looked down at her. She recognised the look that had come into his eyes; her heart started to beat a little faster and she began to edge towards her door. 'You've had a few things on your mind today.'

She nodded, then froze as he reached out his hand, thinking he was going to cup her face again as he had when they'd been dancing. Instead he merely pushed a stray wisp of hair out of her eyes. 'After all,' he said softly, 'it isn't every day your boyfriend goes off and leaves you in the lurch, is it?'

She wanted to say that her absent-mindedness over the tickets had been nothing to do with Gary, that it had had more to do with the fact that he, Liam, had suddenly moved into her family home, but just in time she thought better of it and managed to stop herself. Heaven only knew what he would make of such an admission, and, judging by the look in his eyes, he would need very little on those lines by way of encouragement.

Then, even while she was wondering how best to make her escape, he quite suddenly leaned towards her, and in spite of all her worries as to how she would cope if this very situation were to arise, and in spite of all her previous good intentions, she felt powerless to stop him.

If was as if the same dreamlike state which had possessed her while they had danced had returned, a state of unreality where the consequences of her actions would not matter.

Helplessly she closed her eyes.

Her anticipation was short-lived, however, for his kiss when it came was the merest brushing of his lips, not on hers but on her forehead. She opened her eyes, saw his smile, his hand raised in a goodnight gesture, then he was gone, the door of his flat shutting behind him, leaving her with a sense of bitter disappointment.

CHAPTER EIGHT

SARAH spent a confused and restless night, angry with herself for the way she was reacting to Liam. No doubt he had found her behaviour amusing, especially since it had been she who had gone to such lengths to make it plain that if she went with him to the party there were to be no strings attached.

She had most likely completely misinterpreted his attitude towards her while they had been dancing, and it was more than likely that he acted in that fashion with any girl he happened to be with.

And yet. . .she tossed and turned as sleep eluded her. . .she could have sworn that they had shared some special moments.

But why was she thinking in this way?

Desperately she thumped her pillow. Even if there had been special moments she couldn't do anything about them. She wasn't free to do anything about them; she had Gary to consider.

As her thoughts turned to Gary she wondered where he was. Had he arrived safely in Birmingham? And, if so, was he asleep in some hotel? Maybe he would ring her in the next day or so to tell her what was happening.

It was with that thought in her mind that she finally fell asleep, but her dreams were of a figure on a motorbike who was chasing her through the empty streets. She thought it was Gary, but when she reached the sea-front it was to find the waves crashing across the road and she was unable to pass. When she turned back the figure was removing his crash helmet, and to her dismay it wasn't Gary but Liam who sat astride the machine, and he was laughing at her, although the sound was whipped away by the wind.

Then above the sound of the waves and the howling wind she became aware of another, more persistent sound, and she awoke.

Her bedroom was flooded with sunlight and the mewling sound of gulls filled the air. She lay very still, listening. Had that other sound been part of her dream? But no, there it was again, the sharp crack of some hard object on glass.

Someone was throwing stones at her window.

She scrambled out of bed, padded to the window and parted the curtains. For a moment, because her dream had been so vivid, she half expected to see storm-tossed waves, grey glowering skies and driving rain, but the scene that met her eyes couldn't have been more different.

The vast expanse of water with scarcely a ripple to disturb its surface glittered in the morning sunlight, while black-headed gulls swooped and dived in their quest for food and a lone fishing-boat pulled sedately away from the landing-stage at the end of the pier.

Sarah opened the window, her senses immediately assailed by the fresh tang of the sea air and faintly, in the distance, the sound of church bells.

'You can't still be asleep on this beautiful morning.'

Sharply she looked down. Liam was standing in the garden below. One arm was poised ready to throw another stone at her window. 'It's high time you joined me for training,' he called.

'What training?' she mumbled, noticing that he was wearing a navy blue tracksuit and that his dark hair was ruffled.

'I told you, last night. If we're to do that sponsored walk we have to get some training. Don't you remember?'

'Yes, but I didn't think you meant today. You kept me out half the night, and now you won't even let me have a lie-in.' She glared indignantly at him.

'I'll tell you what — I'm not an unreasonable man.' He regarded her in an amused fashion, his head on one side. 'I'll give you half an hour — no more, mind. I've already jogged along the beach.'

'Jogged?' Sarah looked horrified. 'Who said we had to jog? I thought it was a walk we were doing.'

'All right, in that case we'll go for a walk. Put on some comfortable shoes, but I'm still only giving you half an hour.'

With a grin he was gone, disappearing from her view into the house, and moments later she heard him run up the stairs and let himself into his flat.

Still grumbling, Sarah dragged herself to the shower. Who did he think he was, ordering her around? She could see she would have to have a talk to her new neighbour if he was under the impression that he was going to organise her life in this way. It

had been one thing offering to take her to the party,
it was quite another stipulating how she was to spend
her precious off-duty time.

When she emerged from the shower she grabbed a
cup of coffee and a slice of toast, then pulled on her
old pink tracksuit and worn trainers. As she was
tying the laces she realised she had been hurrying,
and deliberately she slowed down. Even if she had
adopted the 'if you can't beat 'em, join 'em' attitude
where Liam was concerned she certainly didn't
intend to jump to attention at the precise moment he
had stipulated.

When she finally let herself out of the flat there
was no sign of Liam and his door was firmly closed.
She wondered if she should knock, but from the
silence within the flat she had a feeling that he'd
gone out again.

By the time she found him, sitting on the railings
opposite Linfield House and feeding the gulls with
crusts of bread, it was almost forty minutes since she
had caught him throwing stones at her window.

He turned as she approached, his amused gaze
taking in her tracksuit and trainers, but he made no
mention of the fact that she had taken longer than
half an hour. He slid down from the railings and
threw the last piece of bread.

They watched as the gulls circled above them,
scrapping and screaming as if they knew they had
been given the last of the bread.

'So where are we going?' asked Sarah, shielding
her eyes from the bright morning sunlight and staring
at the distant cliffs.

Following her gaze, Liam said, 'I thought we could walk along the beach as the tide is on its way out, take the cliff path into Marcliffe, then backtrack through the woods.'

'That'll take hours,' she protested.

'We've got all day,' he shrugged, and smiled.

She sighed but couldn't be bothered to argue with him, and moments later they were making their way across the fine sand to the hard, wet expanse so recently washed by the tide.

They walked in silence, the imprint of their trainers disappearing immediately in the wet sand as they carefully avoided clumps of seaweed — shiny and brown or skeins of brightest green — and took a route close to the gently lapping waves, parallel to the esplanade.

It was Sarah who broke the silence. 'I love the beach at this time of year, when the tourists have gone home and all you can smell is the ozone instead of fish and chips, sun-oil and ice-cream.'

He laughed then and said, 'What about when you were a child? I would have thought you would have enjoyed the summer then.'

'Yes, I suppose I did, but I was never sorry when it was all over. It's funny, but one of the things I missed the most when I was in London was being near the sea.'

He nodded. 'I know exactly what you mean. It gets into your blood, doesn't it?'

'Were you brought up near the sea?' she asked.

'Yes, my home was on the edge of a small fishing village in Connemara. . .'

'So you do understand.'

He smiled. 'Oh, yes, I understand, although. . .' He paused and stared across the beach to the town, the row of hotels, the restaurants, then turned to look at the pier and lines of upturned pleasure-boats. 'It was very different from this.'

'In what way?' Sarah was curious now, suddenly wanting to know everything about him.

'For a start, we had the Atlantic crashing at our door, and instead of hotels, shops and cliffs we had peat bogs and mountains.'

'It sounds wonderful,' she sighed.

'It is. It's wild and dramatic and it stirs your very soul.'

'What did you do there? Your family—I mean, was your father a fisherman?'

Liam shook his head and smiled as if the idea amused him in some way. 'No, he was a grocer; we ran the only shop in the village.'

'Do you miss it dreadfully?'

He considered her question, staring out to sea, seemingly watching a cross-Channel ferry that had just come into sight on the horizon. 'Yes, at times I suppose I do,' he said at last. 'But only in a nostalgic way. As I said to you before, I think it's a mistake to try to go back. People change. . .'

'So do you never go home?' She was puzzled now.

'Oh, yes, sometimes, of course I do, but only for holidays now.'

Something in the way he said the word 'now' stirred some intuition in Sarah. 'Does that imply that you tried to go back once for something other than a holiday?' she asked.

'You're too perceptive,' he said wryly, then after reflecting for a moment he admitted, 'Yes, you're quite right, I did once think I could go back and pick up where I'd left off.'

'What happened?'

'I was prepared for change—of course I was. I knew I'd find that people had changed, but what I was unprepared for was just how much I'd changed. My world had grown during the years of my training and I suppose I'd grown up. What I'd wanted so intensely at eighteen suddenly was no longer important. Call it the onset of maturity if you like, but whatever it was I wanted more than life in Connemara had to offer.'

'Was there someone special in Connemara?' Sarah asked the question tentatively, afraid that if she probed too deeply Liam would simply change the subject. She was surprised therefore when he seemed willing to talk.

'Of course there was. Her name was Mary. We grew up together.'

'Childhood sweethearts?'

He smiled. 'Something like that, yes. She was a lovely girl, as free and wild as the land in which we lived. We pledged undying love, as children do, but. . .' He trailed off and, glancing at him, Sarah saw a far-away look on his face and she remained silent for a moment, knowing he was back there, his imagination reliving two children playing in that wild landscape.

'It all changed, of course,' he went on. 'She's married now, a local man, a farmer, much older than her. The last I heard she had three children and another on the way.'

'So she didn't wait for you. . .?'

'I doubt it would have made any difference if she had. As I said, the changes were too great. She'd changed, but, more than that, I'd changed.'

They walked on beyond the point where the esplanade ended and the cliffs began, and Sarah found herself wondering at what Liam had said. Had she made a mistake in coming back to her home-town? Had Gary changed while she had been away? But more importantly had she? Was she too realising that life had more to offer than she had once been prepared to settle for?

'That's where we're hoping to have the barbecue.' Liam brought her thoughts back to the present as he pointed to a small cove sheltered by the cliffs. 'The council have given their permission, provided we don't leave any litter.'

'Are you intending to cook on an open fire?' she asked.

'Some things, yes—potatoes, and chestnuts—but we shall use a conventional charcoal barbecue for the meat.'

'I'm looking forward to it,' said Sarah. 'It sounds as if it will be fun.'

'Don't forget the twenty miles you have to walk first.' He grinned at her, and she pulled a face back. 'Anyone who doesn't complete the walk doesn't get a hot dog.' Then, growing serious, he gave her a sideways look. 'Did you enjoy the party last night?'

'Yes. . .'

'You don't sound too sure.'

'Well, it's always a bit difficult when you don't know many people. . .'

'And I suppose your boyfriend not being there made a difference. . .'

'Actually,' Sarah began, then stopped. She had been about to say that her difficulties had not arisen from Gary's absence, but she was afraid Liam might misconstrue that and want to know the real reason, and she could hardly tell him that the difficulty had been with his presence. She threw him a quick glance and saw that he was waiting for her to continue. She swallowed. 'Actually, what I meant was not under-standing all the little intrigues that are going on. You know the type of thing — it happens in any hospital, and the Royal County is no exception. Until you've worked in a place for a few weeks you feel excluded. . .you hear snippets of gossip. . .' She felt herself growing warm under his amused stare and wished she'd never got into this conversation.

'So what gossip have you heard?' he queried.

By this time they were approaching the headland and had turned away from the beach towards the cliffs, their shoes making a crunching sound as they scrambled over a bank of shingle.

Sarah shrugged. 'Oh, the usual thing — who fancies who, nothing too incriminating.'

'Well, you can't have heard too much about me,'

said Liam. 'I've been leading a pretty blameless life recently.'

'Oh, the stories about you have been the worst,' she said solemnly.

'What do you mean?' He stopped and stared at her in mock disbelief. 'It's lies, all of it—I swear it.'

'That's not what I heard.' Sarah had walked on and stopped to wait for him at the foot of a flight of steep steps hewn from the cliff-face. 'In fact, I heard you were responsible for more broken hearts among the nursing staff than any other SHO they've ever had.'

'I tell you, I swear, I'm not guilty.' He pressed his hand to his heart, but there was a smile hovering about his lips. 'I've never broken anyone's heart.'

They'd begun the steep climb up the cliff-face, and Sarah glanced back down at him. 'What about Tina?' she asked.

'Tina?'

'Yes, Tina Mills.'

'What about her?'

Their breathing was becoming slightly laboured now, and they slowed their pace.

'Well, I'd say you were well on the way to breaking her heart.'

'I don't know what you're talking about.'

Sarah paused for breath, one hand on the safety rail, and turned again to look at Liam. She had expected to find the same look of feigned innocence on his face, but instead his expression was one of genuine amazement.

'Don't tell me you didn't know?' she demanded.

'Didn't know what? Sarah, for heaven's sake tell me what you're driving at.'

'Well, apparently Tina's had a crush on you for weeks. I assumed you knew. Everyone else seems to.' She took a deep breath, then, craning her neck, looked up to the top of the cliff and stoically began climbing again.

'I assure you, I had no idea. . .but now you mention it I must admit she does seem to keep appearing, and she's very keen to help with the fund-raising,' Liam admitted.

They climbed the last section of the cliff in silence, then as Sarah reached the top, her breath coming in short gasps, she threw herself down on to the short springy turf just as Liam reached the top step.

He stood for a moment leaning forward, his hands on his thighs. 'Talking of fund-raising,' he said, 'you're going to have to get in better condition than this if you're going to walk twenty miles.'

'Speak for yourself!' Sarah retorted indignantly. 'At least I got to the top before you did!'

He grinned, then lowered himself down beside her and produced two chocolate bars from his pocket. 'Here,' he said, handing her one, 'replace your energy.'

They devoured the chocolate in silence then, turning to Sarah, Liam asked, 'Were you really serious about Tina?'

'Yes, really serious.' Carefully she licked her fingers where the chocolate had melted, stuffed the wrapper in her pocket, then, hugging her knees, stared out to sea.

'I still find it hard to believe — I honestly had no idea.'

'She was pretty angry with me last night, I can tell you,' Sarah told him.

'Why?'

'Because you brought me to the party. I tried to explain that I'd only gone with you because Gary had gone away, but I don't think she believed me.' She glanced curiously at him to see what effect her words were having, but it was difficult to tell, for apart from a slight frown that creased his forehead his face was expressionless, giving away nothing of his feelings. 'Maybe you should have a word with Tina,' she concluded at last.

'Why should I do that?' Liam turned his head, raising his eyebrows in surprise, implying that her suggestion would be the last thing he would do.

She shrugged. 'Well, you could put her out of her misery,' she said weakly, then added, 'One way or another.' As she spoke for some reason she felt a sudden stab of dismay. Quite obviously Liam had been unaware of Tina's feelings towards him. Now she had been the one to enlighten him. Maybe this revelation would be the start of a torrid affair.

But why should it matter to her? What difference should it make? Deep down she knew she was in no position for it to make any difference at all. So if that was the case, why did she feel miserable at the thought of Liam and Tina together?

The next moment, however, all such thoughts were swept from her mind as Liam said, 'Was that the only reason you came to the party with me? Because your boyfriend couldn't go?'

She stared at him. 'You know it was. . . I told you.'

He sighed, then ran his fingers through his dark hair. 'Yes, yes, I know what you told me. . .but we had a good time, didn't we?'

The amused, almost wicked look was back in his dark eyes, the look that made it virtually impossible for her to look away. Finally she was forced to smile. 'Yes, Liam,' she said softly, 'we did have a good time.' She knew he was referring to the dance they had shared and that moment when they had become sexually aware of each other.

'It felt very right, didn't it?' he murmured. 'It made me think that in another time and another place maybe we could have been meant for each other.'

Sarah's heart had begun to beat very fast now. While he had been talking she had leaned back on the grass, supporting her weight on her hands, and suddenly she stiffened as she felt his hand cover one of hers. She made no attempt to withdraw it, however.

'When you were a child, you must have played games of make-belive — I know I did,' he said, and the Irish lilt in his voice was more pronounced than ever, conjuring up images in her mind of him as a small boy in Connemara, where the countryside was wild and the Atlantic pounded on the rocks.

She smiled. 'Of course I did. I was a very imaginative little girl. I always believed my knight in shining armour would come for me.'

'Let's play that game today,' he said, and his voice was full of excitement and of the magic of childhood, as far removed from his role as a senior house officer as it was possible to be.

'But——' she began to protest, some inner voice warning her that there was no telling where this folly could lead.

'No buts. . .' Liam interrupted, taking his hand from hers and placing his fingers against her lips. 'We'll pretend no one else exists. There's only you and me, and the sky and the sea. I'll be your knight, if that's what you want, and you'll be my lady.'

He leaned towards her and, taking his fingers from her lips, covered her mouth with his own. His kiss was light, like the touch of a butterfly, an almost intangible thing, fitting to the fantasy they were playing.

For a moment she pulled back, still hesitating, still unsure about the consequence of such actions, and he, sensing her fear, whispered words of reassurance.

'Just for today, to see what might have been. Tomorrow we return to reality.'

And in that moment Sarah knew that she too wanted to play his game, wanted to find out more about this man who had tantalised her ever since she'd set eyes on him. She too wanted to know what might have been between them if only they'd met in different circumstances. He made it sound an easy game to play, and maybe it would be if she could play it to his rules. . .that for one day no one else existed—no Gary, no memories of Mary, no Tina, no anyone, just themselves and the elements, and then tomorrow a return to normal with no repercussions.

With a sigh she lifted her face to him, closed her eyes and parted her lips.

CHAPTER NINE

LIAM had moved so that he was kneeling beside her on the grass and, as he had done once before, he caught her face between his strong hands, lifting it to him, his thumbs beneath her jaw, his fingers entangled in her hair.

Then as a sudden playful breeze rippled across the cliff-tops, stirring the grasses and blowing tendrils of Sarah's dark hair into her face, she felt his mouth cover hers, and this time his kiss was anything but light. Demanding and possessive, it grew in its intensity, stirring feelings and hidden desires in a way that Gary had never done.

Her own response was just as surprising, and she returned Liam's kisses with a passion that matched his own, winding her arms around his neck, drawing him even closer and burying her fingers in his thick hair.

And when she finally pulled away and opened her eyes all she could see were his own dark eyes, not amused but intense with longing. Everything was forgotten now as raw desire flared between them, controlling both their hearts and their minds.

Then somehow she was lying on the grass and Liam was above her, his mouth claiming hers again, and she was holding him, drawing him closer, straining against him, welcoming the weight of his hard, lean body while at the same time vaguely aware that he was unfastening the top of her tracksuit.

She gasped at the touch of his hand on her breast, then as his fingers teased and caressed and her nipples hardened she arched her back and strained against him, her need every bit as great as his. Then he lowered his head, his mouth taking over from his hands, leaving them free to explore the rest of her body while she moaned with pleasure, unaware of anything save their mutual passion as they rushed headlong past the point of no return.

It was the sound of voices carried by the breeze, high, childish voices, that brought Sarah abruptly to her senses. She stiffened and turned her head sharply, and Liam, sensing her withdrawal, lifted his head.

'What is it?' he said sharply.

'Voices—listen. There's someone coming.' She struggled to sit up, rearranging her clothing as she did so, while Liam cautiously lifted himself so that he could see the footpath that led across the fields away from the cliffs.

'Who is it?' she whispered.

'A party of cub Scouts,' he muttered. 'Would you credit it?'

It was too late for them to move, so they sat upright, looking out to sea, while the group of boys and their leader passed them and began descending the steps to the beach.

As the last two went past Sarah heard one of them snigger, and she felt the colour rush to her cheeks.

They didn't move until they saw the boys running

on the beach far below, then Liam turned to look at her. 'That was a bit unfortunate, wasn't it?' he said softly.

She nodded, but as he reached out to take her hand she turned abruptly away. The magic that had been between them, fragile to start with, had gone, snatched away by the breeze, and suddenly she felt guilty and ashamed.

'What is it?' he asked softly.

'I—don't know. I think we'd better go home.'

'Sarah, I'm sorry, but I. . .'

'No, don't. It was my fault. I should never have agreed to such a game. It was stupid and dangerous.'

'Is that all it was?' he asked. 'A game?'

Sarah stood up and brushed all traces of grass from her tracksuit. 'I'm not sure what it was, Liam, but there's one thing I'm certain of—it should never have happened.'

'You know if they hadn't come along. . .'

'Of course I know.' Her voice rose slightly. 'We'd allowed ourselves to get carried away like a couple of teenagers. Well, Liam, it mustn't happen again.' Suddenly she was aware that she was shaking, but whether from anger or frustration she didn't know. All she knew was that she wanted to get home, shut the door of her flat and be alone.

She turned away from him and began walking, taking the path that led directly down to the town instead of the one they had intended to take across the fields and through the woods.

With a sigh Liam scrambled to his feet and began to follow her.

The path was narrow, forcing them to walk most of the way in single file, then after they'd crossed a stile it opened out and Liam caught her up. In an obvious attempt to lighten the tension between them he threw her a sideways glance and said, 'What about the training?'

'What training?' Her response came out sharper than she had intended. 'This walk wasn't about training, was it, Liam? None of it's been about training. Well, that's the end of it. I thought I could simply be friends with you, but you obviously want more than that, so in future it would be best if we only see each other in a professional way.'

He tried to protest, but she cut him short, and they walked the rest of the way in silence.

The peace she had thought would come with solitude didn't, and for the rest of that day Sarah was tormented by her own thoughts and emotions.

She was angry.

Angry with Liam, whom she believed somehow to have contrived everything that had happened, not only today but ever since she had met him, angry with Gary for going away when she most needed him, but most of all she was angry with herself for allowing herself to be put into such a vulnerable position.

She'd known all along that she was attracted to Liam; she should have seen that as a warning. She should not have gone to a party with him, trying to convince herself that there would be no harm in it. And if that hadn't been enough, as if dancing with him and becoming aware of his appeal weren't sufficient warning, she'd agreed to go on a solitary walk with him.

And somehow, she wasn't even sure how, she'd been drawn into his ridiculous, fantasy game. However could she have allowed that to happen?

And what he had said, of course, was quite true. If those children hadn't come along when they did, incredible as it seemed, she knew they would have made love. Nothing else would have stopped them — that was for sure. Not her conscience, her common sense, or her thoughts of Gary. In fact, she thought guiltily, she hadn't given Gary a second thought while she had been with Liam.

Whatever was the matter with her? She'd never done anything like it before.

But then she'd never before felt the way she had with Liam. He'd stirred something deep inside she'd only been half aware of, and it wasn't only a sexual awareness. Liam had touched some chord in her soul, a chord that had been echoed in his own soul, and she knew he had been aware of it too.

Nevertheless, it was something that had to be curtailed before it had the chance to grow and overwhelm them both.

Sarah was glad to get back to work the next morning.

She had slipped out of the house very early, and as she'd driven away she'd noticed that Liam's light was still on. She knew she would have to face him on the ward, but at least there they would have to be guarded over what they said.

When she arrived it was to find that the morning routine had started, with the patients who had been admitted the previous day being prepared for Theatre.

During report Sarah learnt that Sharon Jesson had been operated on for an ectopic pregnancy and had had a left salpingectomy — one of her fallopian tubes removed.

'She's recovering well and she had a fairly comfortable night,' said Alison May, who had been on duty again that night. 'She had an intravenous infusion of plasma for the first twelve hours and Maxolon for nausea. She's still having Pethidine for pain, and she has a wound drain.' She put Sharon's case file to the bottom of the pile in front of her and looked at the next one.

'Oh, yes,' she said, and her tone changed.

Sarah looked up quickly and caught Alison's eye. 'You were asking about Wanda Firmin, weren't you, Sarah, the other night when you came in? Well, she was fine until about six o'clock last evening when she suffered a heavy vaginal bleed with abdominal pain. She was given a transfusion, but suffered an incomplete abortion and was taken to Theatre. She's Rhesus-negative and she's been given Anti-D. She had a reasonably comfortable night, but she's very distressed this morning.'

Alison carried on down the list of patients, giving details of the new admissions: one patient for dilatation of the cervix and curettage or scraping of the uterus, and one vaginal prolapse repair for a patient whose uterus had dropped into the vagina. There were to be two investigative laparoscopies — one for a patient with pelvic inflammatory disease who had been experiencing pain and feverish episodes and the other for a woman with a history of pelvic pain possibly arising from the presence of adhesions from old scar tissue from an appendectomy. Also on the list were two terminations of pregnancy, one for a mother-to-be who had contracted rubella or German measles in the tenth week of her pregnancy, and the other on a sixteen-year-old schoolgirl. The morning's two major operations were for a hysterectomy being performed for a patient with a heavy menstrual loss and a bilateral oophorectomy, or removal of the ovaries, on a patient experiencing recurrent bouts of inflammation of the ovaries.

'As you can see,' Alison concluded, 'a pretty mixed bag this morning—and the best of luck. I'm off home to bed.'

'What about Ellie Woodmore?' asked Sarah.

Alison paused and looked down at her records again. 'Oh, yes, I missed Mrs Woodmore, didn't I? Well, I'm afraid she's developed a chest infection on top of her other troubles. The day staff moved her into the side-ward yesterday—it's quieter for her in there. The registrar came up to see her and she's had further antibiotics added to her medication, but she had a restless night.'

As they left the office Lucy touched Sarah's arm. 'What did Alison mean about you coming in here the other night?' she queried.

'Nothing much,' said Sarah. 'It was after the party. Liam wanted to call in, that was all.' Noticing the gleam in Lucy's eye, Sarah had started to edge away.

The last thing she wanted was to be dragged into an inquest on the party or an interrogation into what had happened since.

Lucy, however, seemed to have other ideas, and as they made their way to the post-op side of the ward, asked, 'So what happened then?'

'What do you mean, what happened then?' Sarah demanded sharply.

'Well, what happened after you left here? I take it he took you home?'

'Of course he did.' Sarah was about to add that he hadn't had much choice, then she bit her lip as she remembered that Lucy didn't know Liam was living at Linfield House.

'So?'

'So what? Honestly, Lucy, you're the limit. What do you think happened?'

'I don't know,' Lucy grinned. 'You tell me. But if the way he was dancing with you had anything to do with it, I should say——' She broke off as Liam suddenly appeared in the corridor before them, having just stepped out of the lift.

Sarah's heart seemed to turn over as their eyes met, then he gave a cool nod, and, quite unlike his usual self, strode past them to the office.

They watched him in silence, then Lucy said in amazement, 'What's up with him this morning?'

'I've no idea,' replied Sarah, 'but maybe that answers your question for you.' She hurried on to the ward, relieved to have escaped from Lucy's ridiculous innuendoes, but at the same time conscious of feeling hurt by Liam's coolness.

But why should she feel hurt? she chided herself as she prepared to give Sharon Jesson her bed-bath, for hadn't she made it quite plain to Liam that this was the way she wanted things? That from now on there was to be no familiarity between them and that their only relationship was to be a professional one?

The day had got off to a bad start, and as the morning progressed it seemed to go from bad to worse. The gossip among the staff was of Helen's party, and Sarah tried to avoid it as much as she could.

She spent as much time as she could spare comforting Wanda Firmin, who, finding it difficult to accept the fact that she'd lost her baby, had found out that one of the patients for Theatre that day was to have a termination.

Sarah asked her gently how she knew, and Wanda went on to say that the girl herself had told her.

'Blasé about it, she was,' she sniffed between sobs.

'She has her reasons,' said Sarah, taking the woman's hand in hers and squeezing it silently, relieved that Wanda didn't know that there were in fact two terminations on the list that morning. 'And they'll be very good reasons.'

'But it's so unfair.' Wanda groped for a tissue and wiped her eyes, already red and swollen. 'We've waited years for this baby. . .'

'I know, Wanda, I know. And there'll be others, believe me. At least now you know you can conceive. You were never sure before, were you?'

'But why did it have to die?' sobbed Wanda.

'Sometimes it's nature's way of saying that child

wasn't meant for this world. Maybe it wouldn't have been able to cope with life.'

Wanda had been about to blow her nose, but she stopped, the tissues halfway to her face, and stared at Sarah. 'You mean it might have been handicapped?'

'Who knows?' said Sarah. 'I'm just trying to suggest reasons. Now I want to take your blood-pressure.'

When Sarah left Wanda after checking her blood-pressure and blood loss she was pleased to see that she seemed a little calmer, and she drew back the curtains from around her bed.

As she left the ward she saw Sister approaching with the doctors to do their morning round, and she noticed that Liam was with them, which meant he wasn't in Theatre that morning.

Quickly Sarah made her way to the treatment-room to prepare some dressing trolleys. She didn't feel ready to face Liam again yet, and especially not on a ward round.

When she had finished the trolleys she slipped into the sluice which adjoined the treatment-room to wash her hands, and it was while she was drying them that she heard someone come into the treat-ment-room.

'Come in here, Philip; I want to get this straight now.'

Sarah froze as she recognised Liam's voice, but it wasn't his usual easygoing tones, and she immedi-ately realised he had brought the junior doctor into the privacy of the treatment-room for some sort of reprimand. Before she had the chance to step out of the sluice, however, Liam had continued talking.

'Am I to understand that you rode your motorbike home after the party on Saturday night?'

'Yes, Liam. . . Yes, Dr O'Neill,' Philip corrected himself.

'But when I asked you, at the party, you said you were going to leave your bike there and walk home.'

'Yes, I know I said that. But I changed my mind.'

'Why did you do that?'

Silence followed Liam's question, and Sarah found herself holding her breath. There was no way now she could make her presence known and embarrass Philip any further.

At last he mumbled an answer. 'I. . . I took Tina. . .Nurse Mills home.'

'But you'd been drinking.' Liam's voice was like ice.

'Yes. . .yes, I know.'

'So why did you take such a stupid risk?'

Another silence followed, and Sarah could imagine Philip red-faced with embarrassment.

'For God's sake, Philip, I credited you with more sense. Not only did you put your own life at risk and that of your passenger, but the lives of any unfortunate souls you may have encountered on the way.'

'I hadn't had that much to drink. . .' protested Philip.

'How much?' demanded Liam.

'I don't know exactly. . .about three pints of lager. I suppose.'

'So you'd have been over the limit. You were

breaking the law, and if you'd been stopped and
breathalysed you'd have been charged, fined, and
banned from driving. What made you act in such an
irresponsible manner?'

'Nurse Mills was upset,' Philip muttered.

'What about?'

Sarah caught her breath. Was Philip about to
confirm what she'd told Liam the previous day — that
Tina had a crush on him and that no doubt she'd
been upset by his behaviour towards her, Sarah?

'It was a personal matter,' said Philip at last.

'Well, get your act together, Dr Taylor, and stop
putting your career at risk.'

Sarah heard the sharp click of the treatment-room
door, followed by silence, and, thinking that both
men had returned to the ward, she stepped cautiously
out of the sluice — only to find Philip still there.

He looked up sharply, his surprise turning to
embarrassment as he realised she must have heard
everything.

'Philip, I'm so sorry,' Sarah apologised. 'I got
trapped in there.'

He shrugged. 'You heard? Oh, well.' He frowned.
'I don't know what's up with him this morning. He's
been like a bear with a sore head; I haven't been
able to do anything right, then when he heard about
my driving home that did it. I knew I shouldn't have
driven really, but Tina was upset and she didn't want
to walk, so I took a chance. Besides, I expect he's
taken chances.' He glanced up. 'He drove you home,
didn't he?'

'Yes, Philip, he did, but he doesn't drink,' Sarah said.

'Not at all?' Philip's eyes widened. 'Why not?'

'So that he can drive,' she said simply.

He stared at her for a moment, then sighed and glanced at his watch. 'Well, I suppose I'd better get back, otherwise he'll be having another go at me. I've never known him like this before. Something must have got to him.'

Sarah took a deep breath and followed Philip from the sluice, wondering what he would say if he knew just what it was that had got to Liam.

The day continued to be frantically busy, and she didn't see either Liam or Philip again. Tina didn't come on duty until the late shift, and she made a point of ignoring Sarah.

By the time her shift was drawing to an end Sarah had developed a headache and was looking forward to going home, then a basket of flowers was delivered for Mrs Woodmore, and Sarah took it down to the side-ward where she had been moved.

As she opened the door, however, she paused as she saw Liam was with her. She was about to withdraw when Liam turned his head. 'It's all right, Nurse Bartrum,' he said, and she was relieved to hear that the rough edge had gone from his voice, 'you can come in. I was just leaving.'

He stood up, and briefly his eyes met Sarah's, and for one crazy moment she was back on that cliff-top and they were playing their impossible game.

Then his gaze flickered to the flowers she was carrying and the moment was gone. 'Look, Ellie,' he

said softly. 'Someone's sent you flowers.' He winked
at the old lady in the bed then slipped from the
room.

'He's a lovely man, isn't he, Nurse?' Ellie smiled.

'Yes, Ellie, he is,' agreed Sarah.

'Who are the flowers from? You read the card,
dear, I haven't got my glasses on.'

'It says, "Get Well Soon, Gran. All our love, Rod,
Karen, Scott and Kylie."'

'That's my grandson and his family.' Ellie smiled
proudly, then was racked by a sudden bout of
coughing.

Sarah placed the flowers on her table then
attended to Ellie, giving her a glass of water, prop-
ping her up higher in bed to ease her breathing, and
sponging her hands and face and brushing the still
thick white hair to make her more comfortable.

By the time she had finished, her shift was over,
and thankfully she made her way to the staffroom,
taking off her cap as she went and shaking her hair
loose from its pins. Lucy was in the staffroom, and
Sarah offered her a lift home.

Moments later the two girls were in Sarah's car,
heading out of the hospital grounds.

'Phew, what a day!' gasped Lucy. 'Talk about
Monday blues—I don't know what was wrong with
everyone. As if a full theatre list isn't enough,
without people being edgy as well.'

'Maybe it was simply that—the full theatre list that
got to everyone,' suggested Sarah, knowing full well
that wasn't strictly true, but not wanting Lucy to
probe too deeply.

They drove on in silence for a while, then Lucy said, 'Have you done anything about training yet for this walk?'

'Er — no, not exactly,' Sarah admitted.

'Well, some of us girls are doing a walk tomorrow after work. Do you want to join us?'

'Yes, I think that might be a good idea,' said Sarah. She knew there was no chance that she would complete a twenty-mile walk without some practice, but she knew she mustn't go with Liam again.

'Have you managed to get any sponsors yet?' asked Lucy.

'Yes, a few. My parents agreed to sponsor me before they went away, and also the tenants in the other flats at home.'

'Good. Tina said the demand for sponsor forms was better than we'd hoped. Perhaps that'll cheer Liam up.' Lucy paused as Sarah brought the car to a halt outside her house, then added, 'He certainly needed something to cheer him up today; I don't know what was wrong with him. I've never seen him like that before.'

She got out of the car, and Sarah, sensing she was going to ask more questions, said quickly, 'I'll see you tomorrow, Lucy,' then, letting out the clutch, she accelerated and moved swiftly away.

That evening she was restless, unable to settle to anything, and to her annoyance she found herself wondering if she should talk to Liam, try to explain in some way why she had acted as she had, try to make him realise that she simply wasn't free to embark on the type of relationship he obviously had in mind. What had happened between them had clearly upset him, if the comments of his colleagues regarding the unusualness of his mood were anything to go by.

She knew he was working a long shift at the hospital, and as the evening dragged on she found herself listening for the sound of his footsteps on the stairs.

It was late, nearly eleven-thirty, when she finally heard the sound of his key in his lock.

She moved quickly across to her own door and had just stretched out her hand to open it when her phone rang. She jumped, startled by the unexpectedness of it, hesitated, then, with a muttered exclamation, hurried back across the room to answer it.

CHAPTER TEN

THE call was from Gary, and as she listened while he told her about the opening of the new depot Sarah heard Liam shut his door.

She sighed and tried to concentrate on what Gary was saying. 'It's really fantastic, Sarah. I've never seen one like it — it has absolutely everything.'

'What, the new depot?' she asked in bewilderment.

'No, not the depot, this new sports centre.'

'What sports centre?'

'I told you a moment ago — it's just down the road from the depot, and it really is superb. That's where I've been this evening; that's why I'm so late phoning.'

'Oh, I see. So how's the depot going?'

'The depot? Oh, that's the same as the others; it just happens to be in Birmingham, that's all,' said Gary.

'So when will you be home?'

'I'm not sure yet, probably next week some time. I must go now; my money's running out — I'm phoning from the hotel foyer. Oh, are you OK, Sarah?' The pips sounded.

'Yes, I'm fine.'

The line went dead, and Sarah stared at the receiver before replacing it. Slowly she stood up and looked at the door, but suddenly she felt she could no longer approach Liam and say what she had been going to say.

For the rest of the week Sarah and Liam continued to avoid each other, and when they were forced to converse the mood between them remained cool. With the rest of the staff, however, Liam seemed to have resumed his usual charming manner, and as the week wore on Sarah was forced to admit she missed him. Her misery grew as she watched him talking and laughing with the others.

She hadn't realised just how much time they'd been spending together since she'd joined the staff. Somehow Liam had contrived to take coffee-breaks with her, and every day he had joined her in the canteen for lunch, but now she seldom saw him. At home she usually left before him in the mornings, and he didn't return to his flat until late, usually after she was in bed.

The person who seemed most delighted by all this was Tina Mills, and Sarah saw her on a couple of occasions in animated conversation with Liam. Philip Taylor, on the other hand, seemed almost as miserable as she did, and Sarah guessed he had become fond of Tina.

On the ward Wanda Firmin went home, followed a couple of days later by Sharon Jesson. Six more patients were admitted, and there were four emergencies. There was talk of moving Ellie Woodmore to a medical ward as the bed situation on Gynae became desperate.

Sarah had sold almost all the tickets for the barbecue, and she joined the other girls on two occasions for training walks.

After the second of these training sessions a group of the staff ended up in the social club. Sarah found a table, while Lucy went to the bar to get their drinks, then out of the corner of her eye she saw Tina making her way through the crowded bar towards her. As Tina generally went out of her way to avoid her Sarah looked up in surprise, her eyes narrowing when she saw the angry expression on the other girl's face.

'What is it with you?' Tina hissed.

'What are you talking about?' Sarah frowned.

'Just how many men do you need?' There were two bright spots of colour on Tina's usually sallow cheeks.

'I beg your pardon!'

'You went to great lengths at that party, for some reason of your own, to tell me that you had a boyfriend — didn't you?' Tina demanded.

'I mentioned I have a boyfriend, yes. . .but. . .' Sarah began.

'Then how do you explain the fact that you're living with Liam O'Neill?'

'What?' Sarah gaped at Tina.

'Don't try and deny it. I suppose you think you've been very clever pretending to ignore him recently, but don't think I haven't noticed.'

'Tina, you've got it wrong. . .' Sarah began, aware that Lucy had returned to the table and that others in the club were looking in their direction.

'Have I?' demanded Tina. 'Then explain that!'

It was then that Sarah realised Tina had been clutching a sheet of paper to her chest, and as she finished speaking she slammed it on the table. As she looked down Sarah recognised the list of names and addresses of people wishing to take part in the sponsored walk which Tina had been collecting.

'Whatever's going on?' Lucy set the glasses down and stared from Tina to Sarah in amazement.

'There!' Tina, ignoring Lucy, pointed to a line near the top of the list that read, 'Sarah Bartrum, Linfield House,' then, moving her finger down the list, she stopped at a name right at the bottom: 'Liam O'Neill, Linfield House'.

'She doesn't have to explain anything.' Lucy, who had been reading over Tina's shoulder, leaned forward, coolly picked up the list and thrust it back at Tina. 'Just clear off, Tina, and take your grubby little list with you.'

Tina stood for a moment glaring at them both, then she turned on her heel and marched out of the club, amid amused stares from the other occupants, who when they realised that the drama was over carried on with their conversations.

Sarah, who had half risen out of her chair, sank back and stared at Lucy in dismay. 'I wish you'd let me explain,' she muttered.

'Why should you? It's got nothing to do with her who you choose to live with.'

Lucy sounded so indignant that it was almost comical, and Sarah, in spite of her dismay, was forced to smile as Lucy threw her a curious glance.

'But you'd like to know if it's true, is that it?'

'Not if you don't want to tell me. As I said, it's got nothing to do with anyone else.' Lucy sniffed, then took a sip of her drink. 'If you and Liam have chosen to live together. . .'

'But that's the whole point — we haven't — I mean, we aren't,' protested Sarah.

'But the address. . .?'

'Linfield House is my family home, but it's in flats now. I have one, Liam has another, it's as simple as that, but I don't like the idea of Tina going off with the wrong impression.'

'It'll do her good,' said Lucy unsympathetically. 'I'm sick of her mooning about Liam O'Neill all the time. She's wasting her time, especially when his interests seem to be elsewhere. . .' She threw Sarah a speculative look.

'Aren't you forgetting something?' Sarah reminded her. 'I already have a boyfriend.'

'Oh, yes, the elusive Gary.'

'What do you mean elusive?'

'Well, he doesn't seem to be very much in evidence, does he?'

'I told you——' Sarah sighed '— he's away at the moment.'

'Oh, yes, that's right — Birmingham, isn't it? I expect you'll be glad when he gets back.'

Later as she drove home Sarah asked herself that very question. Would she be glad when Gary got back? For the first time she found herself wondering.

During the last few days the calm weather had changed, giving way to high winds and squally bursts of rain, and as Sarah drove along the wind-swept esplanade she noticed that the sea was a heaving angry mass, while the wind had blown sand across the road which had drifted like snow into great mounds against the buildings. It was fairly typical weather for the time of year, but she found herself hoping it would change again before the sponsored walk and the barbecue the following week.

She let herself into her flat, and by the time she'd showered and changed into jeans and a loose top the wind had risen even more and was howling around the house, to such an extent that it was almost impossible to hear anything else.

It was during a lull when the wind seemed to be mustering itself for another onslaught that Sarah thought she heard a knock at her flat door. She was in her kitchen at the time, looking in her fridge and wondering what she could have for supper. She straightened up and listened, then, thinking she'd imagined it, that it was simply the wind causing something to bang about outside, she carried on with what she was doing.

Then the sound came again, and this time there was no mistaking it. There was definitely someone knocking.

Closing the fridge, she hurried through her sitting-room and pulled open the door.

Liam, dressed in a trench coat, its collar upturned against the weather, was leaning against the door-frame, one arm supporting a large brown paper bag.

The old amused expression that she had come to know so well, but which had been missing recently, was back in his eyes. She felt as if her heart had turned over and for a moment she was unable to speak.

'I thought it was probably my turn to get supper.' He said it solemnly, but there was laughter in his eyes. 'I hope you like Chinese.' He glanced down at the paper bag.

'I love it.' She was smiling now, smitten by his irresistible smile.

'So aren't you going to ask me in? On the other hand, you could come into my lair. . .'

Hurriedly she stood aside, and as he strolled into her flat she closed the door behind him. She followed him into the kitchen, where he set his package down. 'This is still pretty hot, so if you'd like to get some plates.'

But Sarah was still staring at him, bemused by his unexpected appearance.

He glanced up and, seeing her expression, said, 'What's wrong? Aren't you hungry? Don't tell me you've already eaten.'

'No, no,' she said quickly.

'Then what?' His expression was quizzical now, his head on one side, but the suppressed laughter still simmered beneath the surface.

'What did you mean when you said it was probably your turn to get supper?' Sarah asked.

'Isn't that what couples do, take it in turns to do the chores?'

She frowned. 'Couples? The chores?'

'Yes, when they live together.'

She stared at him, then as it slowly dawned on her what he meant she turned away with a slight groan.

'It's all over the hospital, you know, that you and I are living together,' Liam told her. 'I tried denying it, but no one would believe me, so in the end I thought, What the hell? If that's what they want to think, let them think it. Besides, I'm fed up with us not being friends.'

'So am I,' Sarah whispered.

'Truce?' He raised his eyebrows.

She nodded. 'Truce.'

'I've missed you,' he said, while she took plates from the cupboard and he began to undo the foil containers of food. 'I'd got so used to us having lunch together, talking. . .just being together and—well, to tell the truth, I've been thoroughly miserable, especially thinking you're still mad at me.'

'I'm not still mad at you.' Sarah shrugged helplessly.

'You mean you've missed me too?'

'I didn't say that. . .'

'Not just a little bit?' Liam held up his finger and thumb about an inch apart, and she was forced to laugh.

'All right, just a little bit.' Sarah took cutlery from a drawer and they sat down opposite each other at her pine bench table. She knew it was true. She had missed his company dreadfully, but she wasn't sure she should admit it. She wasn't sure how he would interpret such an admission.

They ate in silence for a while, but Sarah's mind was racing. She was pleased Liam had come, pleased they were friends again. But what would happen next? The circumstances between them were still the same as they had been the day she had walked away from him on the cliffs.

Almost as if he could read her thoughts Liam broke the silence. 'I blew it, didn't I?'

'Blew it?' She knew what he was referring to, but she was playing for time.

'Yes, that day on the cliffs. I'm sorry, Sarah, really I am. You were quite right; it really was a stupid game to play. You must have thought I was some sort of crazy pervert.'

She shook her head. 'No, Liam, I didn't think that at all.'

'But you thought I'd contrived everything. . .the training. . . You said so.'

'I know I did, and I'm still not convinced that you didn't.' She glanced at him, but there was an innocent look on his face. 'But it wasn't so much that. . .it was what happened afterwards, and I know I was as much to blame for that as you were.'

'So why do you think it happened?' he asked softly a little later as he finished eating and pushed his plate away.

'I don't know, Liam. I can't explain it. . .'

'I can't imagine you're in the habit of behaving like that with someone you've only met a week or so before.'

'Of course I'm not,' she cried indignantly. 'It's never happened before. . . I've never felt like that before.'

'Ah,' he said knowingly. 'Perhaps we're getting somewhere now.'

'What do you mean?' she demanded.

'Well, you say you only acted like that because your feelings were different from anything you'd felt before?'

'Yes. . . I suppose so.'

'So your actions were quite spontaneous?'

'Yes. . .'

'So what we need to know is why you felt the way you did.'

'Why only me?' she demanded. 'Why all the interest in my feelings? What about your feelings? You were there too.'

'Ah, but my feelings aren't in question. I apologised for my actions, not my feelings.' Liam stood up, and before she had the chance to move leaned across the table and kissed the tip of her nose. 'There's no doubt about my feelings, Sarah.' He gazed into her eyes as he spoke. 'I know exactly what I felt and why.'

Flustered now by the look in his eyes, she stood up, collected their plates and took them to the sink. 'I think I'd better make some coffee,' she said. 'I take it you'd like some?'

'I'd love coffee.'

He leaned against the work-top watching her as she filled the percolator and switched it on. He'd removed his jacket and tie before they sat down; now he turned back the cuffs of his shirt, and as Sarah caught sight of the dark hair that covered his arms she felt something stir inside her, and, recognising it as being dangerously similar to the desire she'd felt for him before, she looked quickly away. She mustn't start feeling like that again, she thought desperately. She had to keep the mood light between them at all costs, but judging by the look on Liam's face she knew it wasn't going to be easy.

They took their coffee into the sitting-room, and Sarah deliberately sat in an armchair, leaving Liam to sit alone on the sofa, and in an attempt to keep the conversation as superficial as possible she said, 'So how did you hear that we were living together? Did Tina demand an explanation from you?'

'Tina? No, why should she?'

'She did from me,' she told him.

'But why should she do that?' He looked puzzled.

'I told you—she has a crush on you. She seems to think you're her exclusive property.'

'You don't seem to have so much sympathy for her now,' he said drily.

'No, I haven't,' she admitted. 'In fact, she annoyed me.'

'But why did she think we were living together?' he asked.

'It was that list she got up for the sponsor forms— it seems we'd both put our address merely as Linfield House. Tina, in the suspicious way she has over anything remotely connected with you, simply jumped to conclusions.' Sarah frowned suddenly and set her mug down. 'But if Tina didn't say anything, how did you know? Did you see Lucy?'

'Lucy?' he queried.

'Yes, she was with me when Tina attacked me in the social club.'

He laughed then. 'No, it wasn't Lucy. But I think I must have gone into the Club just after you left. I would imagine that others who were in there must have heard what had been said. Anyway, I came in for some ribbing from some of the other housemen. Young Philip Taylor even congratulated me, but even that makes sense now—I've heard he has a thing about Tina Mills. Well, maybe she'll leave me alone now and transfer her affections to Philip.'

'But aren't you forgetting something?' asked Sarah.

He looked up swiftly. 'What do you mean?'

'None of it's true. They'll all have to be told that we aren't living together.'

'Maybe we could remedy that?'

'Don't be silly, Liam, of course we couldn't.'

'Why not?'

'Oh, for goodness' sake, how many more times do I have to say it? I have a boyfriend.'

'Is he the only reason?'

'I'd have thought that was reason enough,' she said in exasperation.

'Would it be different if you didn't have a boyfriend?'

'I don't know. What do you mean?'

'Well, if he weren't on the scene, would I stand a chance?'

She sighed. 'Oh, Liam, that's a hypothetical question.'

'You could still try and answer it.' When she

remained silent he prompted her, 'If you didn't have a boyfriend, could you be interested in me?'

'I think you know the answer to that,' she said quietly, then, seeing the look that flared in his eyes, she added, 'But it doesn't alter anything, does it? I still have Gary. You and I aren't living together, and people will have to be put straight.'

'Couldn't we pretend. . .?'

'No, Liam,' she said sharply, 'no more games!'

'What? Oh, no, I suppose not.' He shrugged. 'Oh, well, I suppose I'll just have to be content with the fact that you'd have been interested in me if you hadn't been committed elsewhere. . .but. . .'

'But what?' Sarah eyed him warily, uncertain what new ploy he was about to try.

'I don't know; correct me if I'm wrong, but I could have sworn that what happened that day on the cliffs —' Then, seeing her expression change, he added hastily, 'Whether it was meant to happen or not, I could have sworn there was something very special between us.'

He was leaning forward now, very close to Sarah, and when she didn't answer he said, 'It was special, wasn't it, Sarah?'

Unable to escape his gaze, she couldn't deny it, knew that to deny it would be a lie, but Liam was waiting, wanting an answer.

'Maybe it was,' she whispered at last, and she heard him sigh, then, pushing away her cup, she stood up and turned away from him, agitated now by the conflict of her feelings.

'Sarah, listen to me,' said Liam urgently. 'If it was

special, if it was more special than what you already
have. . .please think very carefully. You could be
lining yourself up for a lifetime of misery. I know,
remember? It almost happened to me.'

She half turned. 'With Mary?'

'Yes, with Mary. I went away thinking she was the
only girl in the world for me. I now know it would
never have worked—we just weren't right for each
other; we'd have simply made each other miserable.
It has to be right, Sarah.'

He was standing very close behind her now, so
close that she could feel his warm breath on the nape
of her neck, then she stiffened as he put his hands on
her shoulders.

'So do you think you know when it's right?' she
whispered.

'Oh, yes,' he murmured, his lips against her hair.
'I always felt that the moment I met the right woman
I would know. Make no mistake, Sarah, when it's
right, you know.'

Lightly his lips brushed her neck and he drew her
back, holding her against the lean hardness of him.

Her body began to tingle, and suddenly she wanted
him to touch her, to arouse her as he had before.
She wanted to feel his mouth on hers, demanding
and possessing, but above all she wanted him to
make love to her, to carry her to the bedroom and
continue with what he had once started.

She turned and was a fraction of a second away
from slipping into his arms when he abruptly pulled
away.

'Sarah, if it's not to happen again, I must go now.

If I stay any longer I won't be responsible for my actions.'

'But. . .' She stepped forward, on the point of stopping him.

'No, Sarah, not again, not until I'm sure it's what you really want.'

CHAPTER ELEVEN

SARAH spent the rest of that week in an agony of indecision.

She was pleased that she and Liam were friends again, but she was shocked at the strength of her feelings for him. Her awareness of him grew with every passing day, whether it was at work on the wards, in the social club or hospital canteen, or when she lay in bed at night with only a wall dividing them.

She knew he was waiting for her to make some move, but as the week moved rapidly on towards the sponsored walk, the barbecue and Gary's possible return she was no nearer sorting out the tangled mass that her emotions had become.

On the day before the walk Sarah arrived for an early shift to find that once again the shortage of beds on the gynae ward was creating major problems.

'We're going to move Mrs Woodmore to a medical ward,' said Sister Moore during report. 'She's basically recovered from her gynae surgery, but still has breathing problems.'

'She complained of slight chest pain in the night,' said Alison May. 'I called the registrar and he's requested an ECG for this morning.'

'Thank you, Alison,' said Pat Moore. 'I'll get a

houseman to do that, then we'll organise her move. Now, what else do we have?'

Alison carried on with her report, giving details of seven post-op patients, two of whom had been overnight emergencies.

'With six for Theatre this morning there won't be too much sitting around,' said Ria as they left the office.

'My poor feet,' grumbled Lucy. 'I had intended saving myself for tomorrow — fat chance of that now. I see I'm down to do theatre trips this morning.'

'I'm on post-op,' said Sarah. 'I'll go and start with the bed-baths, then I'll get Ellie ready for her move. I'll really miss her, you know; I've got quite used to her being in the side-ward.'

Sarah worked steadily with Kath, the auxiliary nurse, and within half an hour they had the post-op patients ready to face the day.

'I've told Mrs Woodmore we're moving her to another ward,' said Kath as they emptied bowls of water in the sluice.

'How did she take it?' asked Sarah.

'She seemed a bit concerned that her family wouldn't be able to find her when they visited, but I told her I'd phone her daughter and tell her.'

'Well done, Kath. I'll go down to her now that we've finished and get her ready for her ECG.'

'OK,' said Kath. 'Apparently Philip's coming to do that.'

As Sarah left Kath and made her way to Ellie Woodmore's ward she tried to stifle a little pang of disappointment. If Philip was on call it suggested that Liam would be going in Theatre, and as it was Lucy doing theatre trips that morning it meant she wouldn't be seeing him.

With a sigh she pushed open the door of the side-ward, prepared to chat to Ellie and to help her pack up her possessions ready for her move to a medical ward in another part of the hospital. But the sight that greeted her made her freeze in the doorway. Ellie was slumped back against her pillows, her face grey and her eyes rolled back in her head.

Sarah, recovering immediately, started forward, and on reaching the bed took Ellie's hand and felt for a pulse, noting as she did so the blueish colour of the old lady's lips and nails. Her skin felt clammy, she didn't appear to be breathing and there was no sign of a pulse.

In one spontaneous movement Sarah pressed the emergency bell and began to pull Ellie down so that she was flat on the bed.

Other nurses began to arrive in response to the bell, including Sister Moore, who took control, sending one nurse to fetch the emergency box and to phone for the crash team, another to fetch the crash trolley and the auxiliary to go back to the ward to calm the other patients. She then joined Sarah, who had started cardiac massage, and seconds later the nurse arrived with the emergency box containing an airway, and Sister began resuscitation.

Within minutes the crash team arrived, three doctors including Liam, an anaesthetist and two other nurses. Liam seemed to take charge, calling for Lignocaine and Adrenaline to be drawn up while the anaesthetist took over the patient's airway and the oxygen mask, and the nurses began setting up a saline infusion. Monitors were fixed to Ellie's chest, while Sarah kept up cardiac massage, then when she began to tire Liam indicated for Philip to take over.

Sarah stood back and watched, and found herself praying that the old lady would revive. There was, however, no response on the heart monitor screen to their efforts, not even a flicker to indicate any sign of life, and Liam moved forward with the defibrillator pads, calling for the rest of the staff to stand clear.

After the impact Sarah anxiously glanced at the monitor, but the line remained steady.

Two further attempts followed, but with the same outcome. Liam checked for a pulse, then called for the team to stop their efforts.

'That's it, I'm afraid, Sister. I'm sorry.'

'Thank you, Dr O'Neill,' replied Pat Moore quietly.

In the activity that followed, as equipment was dismantled and the crash team prepared to leave, Sarah looked up and found Liam standing by the bed staring down at Ellie.

For a moment she stopped what she was doing and watched him, and it was then, caught in that instant of compassion, that she knew she loved him.

As if he sensed her watching him he looked up, their eyes met, and she couldn't fail to notice the sadness in his.

'I'm sorry, Liam,' she said softly. 'You were fond of her.'

He nodded. 'Yes, I was. She was a grand old lady.'

They stared down at Ellie, peaceful now, her features smooth, the white hair drawn back from her face.

'I don't think I'll ever get used to losing a patient,' he said, then with a brief shake of his head he turned away and left the ward.

At lunchtime there was no sign of Liam in the canteen, and Sarah took her soup and sandwiches to a window-table where she was soon joined by Helen.

'Hi, Sarah—I've been trying to catch up with you all week.' Helen balanced her tray and transferred her lunch to the table then, drawing up a chair, she sat down. 'I say, are you all right?' She peered anxiously at Sarah. 'You look a bit peaky.'

'Oh, I'm OK,' sighed Sarah. 'Just having a bad day on the ward, that's all.'

'So it wouldn't be anything to do with a certain SHO?' asked Helen casually as she peeled the cling-film wrapping from her sandwiches.

'What do you mean?' Sarah looked up sharply.

'Oh, come on, Sarah, you can't play the innocent much longer, and certainly not with me—I know you, remember? Besides, rumour has it that you and Liam are living together.'

'Then rumour has it wrong.' It came out sharper than Sarah had intended, and Helen threw her a quizzical look.

'I must admit I was sceptical when I heard it,' said Helen. 'If it was true I thought you might have told me about it. So how did the rumour start?'

Sarah sighed and explained about the flats, and

Helen nodded thoughtfully. 'I wondered if it was something like that. . .and yet. . .' She hesitated.

'And yet what?'

'I still had the impression there was something between you and Liam O'Neill.'

'Why should you think that?'

'Oh, I don't know — little things, like the way he looks at you, for a start. Then at the party, remember, he asked me questions about you?'

'Did he?' Sarah looked up in surprise. 'What sort of questions?'

'Oh, just ordinary sort of things, about when we were younger and when we were at school together. . .and then lately, I don't know, you've seemed different somehow, preoccupied; in fact if I didn't know better I'd say you were. . .' Helen hesitated.

'You'd say I was what?' Calmly Sarah set her mug down on the table and stared at her friend, aware that her heart was thumping.

Helen laughed. 'I'd say you were in love. . .' She stopped, then glanced enquiringly at Sarah and, catching sight of her expression, said softly, 'Are you, Sarah? Are you in love with Liam?'

'I think I must be. But how can I be, Helen? Oh, I'm in such a muddle.'

Helen stared at her thoughtfully for a moment then, leaning forward slightly across the table, she said, 'You mean because of Gary?'

Sarah nodded miserably.

'So how do you feel about Gary?'

'I don't know. I really thought I loved him.'

'And now?' queried Helen.

'I don't think I do; in fact, I'm sure I don't. I'd even go so far as to say that I doubt that what I did feel for him really was love.'

'Because now you've found out what love really is?'

Sarah nodded again. 'Something like that, yes.'

'And Liam—do you think he feels the same way about you?'

'I think so, but even if he doesn't I know I can't go on with Gary any more.' Sarah glanced ruefully at Helen. 'You tried to warn me that something like this might happen, didn't you?'

Helen gave a tight little smile. 'I just felt that you and Gary might have simply become a habit with each other, and I thought that since leaving home you might have changed.'

They fell silent, and Sarah reflected how Helen's words echoed what Liam had said—how one couldn't go back and expect things to be the same.

'You'll have to tell Gary,' said Helen at last. 'And it will only be then, when that relationship is finished, that you'll be able to discover your true feelings for Liam and his for you.'

'Yes, I know,' sighed Sarah. 'I dread doing it, Helen. I don't want to hurt Gary. I've been fond of him for a very long time.'

'You'll hurt him far more if you stay with him and live a lie,' commented Helen, then added. 'Besides, have you thought things may have changed for him as well? Has he seemed any different since you came back?'

'I'm not sure. . .although at times I didn't think we were so close as we'd been before. And it's bothered me that we seem to have so little in common now.'

'When will you tell him? Is he still away?' asked Helen.

'Yes.'

'Could you phone him?'

Sarah shook her head and stood up. 'No, it's not the sort of thing I should say over the phone. I'll tell him when he comes home.'

Talking to Helen had made Sarah feel better. She had been able to get her emotions sorted out, and once she had made her decision she felt easier in her mind, although she still dreaded having to face Gary and tell him their relationship was at an end.

She was kept busy on the ward for the rest of the day with the post-op patients as they returned from Theatre and were put on to half-hourly observations.

But there was a subdued feeling on the ward following Ellie's death, for everyone, from the nursing staff to the domestics, had become fond of her. Sarah hadn't seen Liam again that day, and as her shift ended she was thankful that it was time to go home.

'All set for tomorrow?' asked Lucy as they changed out of their uniforms.

'Just about,' Sarah nodded. 'I hope the weather's fine.'

'Well, if the rain stops it'll be something.'

As Sarah drove home she noticed that the rain,

which had kept up all day, did seem to be dying out and the sky, far out to sea above the horizon, was a pale turquoise.

The space outside Linfield House where Liam parked his car was empty, and Sarah guessed he must once again be working a long shift. Even at the thought of him her heart seemed to turn over, but she knew she mustn't build her hopes too much where he was concerned. Although he seemed more than interested in her she didn't yet know just how far that interest went. In the past he'd had the reputation of a heartbreaker, and Sarah wanted to be sure before she rushed headlong into another relationship. But, as she'd explained to Helen, she knew that even if things didn't work out with Liam she couldn't continue with Gary.

With Liam she'd had a brief glimpse of how a relationship should be, of how she should feel when a man touched her and of how she should respond when he kissed her.

How she would react when he made love to her she as yet had no idea; she could only imagine how it would be — and how many times during the long hours of the night had she done just that, allowed her imagination to run riot while Liam O'Neill made love to her?

She let herself into the house, and on the hall table found she had some mail. She flicked through the envelopes as she made her way slowly up the stairs — a couple of bills and a circular, a postcard from her parents showing a sunset over a tropical beach, and a plain white envelope.

Her breath caught in her throat as she turned it over, saw a Birmingham postmark and recognised Gary's handwriting.

It was so unusual for him to write when he could phone that she tore it open immediately, not even waiting until she'd taken off her coat. Inside was one single sheet of paper covered in Gary's round, untidy handwriting.

Dear Sarah,

I'm really not sure how to tell you this, so I thought it might be better if I were to write, instead of phoning, as I don't know when I shall see you again. The thing is, I've decided not to come home. Remember the sports centre I told you about? Well, they've offered me a job as an instructor. It's the sort of thing I've always wanted to do, and I can't let the opportunity pass. My parents will be furious, I know, but I can't help it. I was fed up working for Dad; I feel I've missed out somewhere, and I want to do something else with my life.

I'm sorry, Sarah. I'm pretty certain you won't want to come to Birmingham; you seem happy with your new job at the hospital. I hope we can still keep in touch. . .

There were a few more lines, but Sarah let the letter fall as she sank down on to a chair.

She sat for a long time staring out across the sea watching the sky deepen from turquoise to indigo as the dusk gathered, then she stood up, walked through to the sitting-room and, sitting down at her bureau, took out a sheet of paper and a pen and began to write a letter to Gary.

The next morning dawned crisp and clear after a slight overnight frost. A light mist over the sea cleared early and the October sun struggled through.

Sarah, warmly clad in a thick polo-necked jumper, her pink tracksuit, leg-warmers and a pair of stout walking shoes, had just finished a second cup of coffee when she heard a knock on her door.

'I see you're ready.' Liam smiled at her from the doorway, and her heart turned over at the look in his eyes. 'Come on, I'll give you a lift to the hospital.'

'I should make the most of this if I were you,' he said moments later as they climbed into his MG. 'It's Shanks's pony from now on.'

'At least it isn't raining.' Sarah pulled a face.

'That's true, but the going could be soft in places, after all the rain we've had. Just take it easy, Sarah; remember it isn't a race — at least not for you it isn't.'

'What do you mean?' She glanced curiously at him, her pulse racing slightly as she took in his handsome, clear-cut profile, the unruly dark hair and the strong, shapely hands on the steering-wheel.

'Some of the housemen have a wager with the porters as to who'll finish in the shortest time — the money going to the appeal.'

'So you'll be walking with the other housemen?' queried Sarah.

''Fraid so.'

She was disappointed — she had hoped she could walk with him, but when they joined the crowd in the hospital grounds she was quickly drawn into a group that included Helen and Lucy, and as the hospital administrator fired the starter's pistol and the men were away at a cracking pace she was glad she wasn't with them.

'They won't keep that up,' muttered Lucy. 'You see — they'll be straggling later. We'll probably overtake them, like the tortoise and the hare.'

'I shouldn't count on it,' chuckled Helen. 'I say, is that Tina walking with the men?'

'I wouldn't be a bit surprised,' said Lucy. 'She's probably tied herself to Liam.'

'More likely to Philip,' laughed Helen, then, seeing Lucy's surprised expression, she said, 'You obviously haven't heard. Apparently Philip's been besotted with Tina for some time, but she didn't want to know because she only had eyes for Liam. Well, Tina must have got wind of the fact that Liam's interests lay elsewhere and gave up, and that's where Philip stepped in. He told me this morning they've been out a couple of times now.'

'I can't see it lasting,' commented Lucy darkly. 'They're so different.'

'Well, we shall see. Often it's a case of opposites attracting. . .don't you agree, Sarah?' Helen said.

Sarah, who had been silent until that point, nodded and smiled. 'Yes, but I hope Philip doesn't get hurt.'

'He's a big boy now,' said Lucy firmly, 'and it's high time he was able to take care of himself — mind you, he may have bitten off more than he can chew with Tina. I'm just amazed she's given up on Liam.'

'She knew she didn't stand a chance against the competition,' chuckled Helen, and as Lucy took her meaning she grinned at Sarah.

'I can't think what you mean,' said Sarah, but she smiled at the other two girls as she said it. She'd already decided not to tell either Helen or Lucy about her letter from Gary until after the walk.

The circular route for the sponsored walk stretched far beyond the hospital, through miles of winding country lanes between hedgerows thick with hips and berries and tumbling with old man's beard, then meandered across open countryside and through woodland to a pub where the walkers would stop for lunch. Finally the route covered the steep road to the downs, then after crossing the crest joined the path that ran along the cliff-tops and down into the town.

As they tramped through the golden autumnal glory of the woods and approached the pub which would indicate the halfway point of the walk, Sarah wondered if Liam would still be there. But although the low-beamed bar was packed with other walkers there was no sign of Liam or the group he'd been walking with.

They passed Kath on her way out and she waved to them.

'How are the feet?' she called.

'OK,' they laughed, before collapsing thankfully on to the pub benches to rest.

'The worst part will be when we get up again,' grumbled Lucy a little later after they'd eaten a ploughman's lunch.

'I was just thinking that,' admitted Sarah.

'I don't think my feet belong to me,' said Helen.

'My calves hurt more than my feet.' Sarah leaned over to massage the backs of her legs.

'Well, it's no good sitting here moaning; we've got a long way to go yet.' Lucy sighed, stood up, then groaned while the other two laughed.

The going was tough on the steep climb to the downs, the path muddy after all the recent rain, and it took all their concentration just to keep their balance.

'I'm glad we're doing this for charity,' muttered Lucy through gritted teeth.

'Why?' gasped Sarah.

'Because people would think we were mad if we were doing it for pleasure.'

They battled on, and it got fractionally easier when they reached the crest of the downs, although they now had a stiff breeze to contend with that stung their cheeks and whipped their hair across their faces.

Several times they were overtaken by other walkers, and once they overtook a pair who looked as if they might be about to give in. Then towards mid-afternoon, just when Sarah was beginning to doubt whether she could walk much further, they reached the top of the cliffs and looked down at the sea, the beach and the town far below them.

'Ah, the home stretch,' sighed Helen. 'It's all downhill now.'

For a moment Sarah was reminded of the last time she had climbed these cliffs. Then she had been with

Liam. She felt her pulses race as she recalled what had followed, and she turned slightly to look down to the spot where it had happened, then she frowned and lifted her hands to shield her eyes from the sun.

'What's happening down there?' she said.

'Where?' puffed Lucy, putting a hand on Sarah's shoulder for support.

Below them lights were flashing, as two vehicles bumped across the fields away from the cliff-edge towards the main road.

A little knot of people who even from that distance were recognisable as some of their own party were watching the vehicles. Then all but two of the group moved on down the path towards the town.

'That's an ambulance,' said Helen. 'But what's the other vehicle?'

'It's the coastguards' cliff rescue service,' said Sarah. 'There must have been some sort of accident.'

They scrambled down the steep pathway, and as they approached the spot they saw that the pair who had stayed were Kath and her friend Jean, who appeared to be having trouble with the laces in one of her walking boots.

'What happened?' called Lucy as they drew nearer.

'We're not really sure,' replied Kath. 'It was all over by the time we got here. But one of the others——' she nodded towards the rest of the group who were almost out of sight by then '—said it was something to do with some boys skylarking around. There was an accident, and apparently Dr O'Neill was involved.'

Sarah felt her mouth go dry. 'What do you mean?' she said urgently. 'How was he involved?'

'I don't know. I tell you, it was all over when we got here, but I heard someone say he'd gone over the cliff.'

'Oh, my God!' Sarah stared at her in horror, while Helen took hold of her arm.

'Steady on, Sarah. . .'

'Is he badly hurt?' gasped Sarah.

'I've no idea. They've all been taken to Casualty . . .the boys and Dr O'Neill.'

'I must go.' Wildly Sarah stared across the fields to the road.

'No,' said Helen quickly, reading her thoughts. 'It'll be quicker to carry on down to the town. . . Sarah, wait for us.'

But Sarah had gone, her tiredness forgotten as she sped, slipping and sliding on the mud, down the cliff-path, her only thought to get to the man she loved.

CHAPTER TWELVE

AFTERWARDS Sarah couldn't remember much about that nightmare trek back to the hospital. She left Helen and Lucy far behind, while details of every cliff rescue she'd ever heard about teemed through her mind. Ever since she was a child, when a boy in her class at school had fallen over the cliff while bird-nesting and had been killed, she had come to dread the sound of the maroon rockets summoning the cliff rescue team. There had been no such sound that day—maybe they used radios or car-phones these days, she didn't know—but there had been no warning for the scene that had confronted them on the cliff-path.

Hardly aware of the pain in her legs or of her sore feet, Sarah stumbled up the hospital drive, taking a short cut across the neatly trimmed lawns to the casualty unit, her heart full of dread at what she might be about to discover.

The reception area was full of people; patients waiting to be seen, relatives waiting for patients, and staff—medical staff, administrative, and ancillary staff. The noise was deafening; voices, clattering, the sound of an approaching klaxon, a baby screaming, while the air was stuffy and it felt unbearably hot.

Sarah hesitated; she didn't know any of the staff

on Casualty, then determinedly she approached the desk.

'Do you have a Dr O'Neill here?' she asked.

The young receptionist barely looked up. 'I don't know.' She turned to her companion. 'Do we have a Dr O'Neill?' She glanced up at Sarah then. 'I'm new here,' she added.

Sarah looked at the other receptionist, who was shaking her head. 'No, no Dr O'Neill — Dr Roberts is the CO, and Dr Shamar is. . .'

'Oh, no, you don't understand,' said Sarah quickly. 'I think Dr O'Neill has been brought in here — there was an accident on the cliffs. . .'

'Oh, that! Yes.' The receptionist nodded, and glanced towards a set of double doors.

'Thank you.' Not waiting to hear more, Sarah dived for the doors, vaguely aware of the receptionists protesting that she couldn't go in there and that she would have to wait her turn.

As the doors swung to behind her she found herself in a wide corridor with more double doors leading off. One of these sets of doors bore the notice 'Treatment-Room'. Sarah hurried towards it and peered through the wire-meshed windows into the room beyond.

Several white-coated figures were grouped around a couch, but all she could see of the patient was his feet. Horribly certain now that the patient was Liam and that it was his bruised and battered body on the couch, she pushed her way through the doors.

Some of the staff turned to see who had come in, others carried on with what they were doing.

Then a charge nurse approached her. 'Can I help you?' he asked, and his gaze flickered beyond her to where one of the receptionists had just appeared, apologising and protesting that it wasn't her fault.

'I'm looking for Dr O'Neill,' Sarah said, then added, 'I'm Staff Nurse Bartrum.'

The expression on the face of the charge nurse changed and he murmured something to the receptionist, who went away complaining about people who didn't explain anything. Then, turning back to Sarah, he glanced down at the tracksuit and leg-warmers. 'Dr O'Neill, you say? He's over there.' He jerked his head in the direction of another couch on the far side of the room, and Sarah swung round, terrified of what she might be about to see.

Liam, still in his navy blue tracksuit, was leaning against the side of the couch, his arms folded, his long legs thrust out in front of him. He was talking to another doctor.

'Someone to see you, Liam,' called the charge nurse, and he looked up.

'Sarah!' He started away from the couch, his pleasure at seeing her quickly replaced by concern as he saw her expression. 'What is it? What's wrong?'

'Liam, are you all right?' She darted forward, oblivious to anyone else in the room.

'I'm perfectly all right. Why?'

'I thought. . . I heard. . .that is —— Oh, Liam, I was told you'd gone over the cliff.'

He grinned then. 'That's right, I did.'

'But I don't understand. . .' Desperately Sarah searched his features.

'I went over after that young fellow.' Liam nodded towards the other couch. She turned and by then could see that the patient was a boy of about thirteen. The staff had cut his jeans away to reveal what appeared to be a badly injured right leg, while his neck was supported by a spinal collar. He was very pale, his eyes were closed and there were smears of blood on his forehead. 'He and his pals were playing around too close to the cliff-edge, he slipped on the mud and fell over,' explained Liam. 'His fall was broken by a ledge of rock that juts out from the cliff-face. If he'd fallen all the way he'd have hit the rocks at the base of the cliff and been killed immediately. One of the other boys had run into town to get help, and when we got there the cliff rescue team and the ambulance had just arrived. The boy appeared to be injured, so I offered to go over to help him. The team lowered me down, and I was able to give him first aid and a pain-killing injection and to get a collar on him before he was brought to the top.'

In spite of the fact that she felt sorry for the boy relief was starting to wash over Sarah, and she did nothing to disguise it. Liam was safe.

Suddenly she realised he was staring at her. 'What is it?' she asked as gradually she became aware of the amused smiles of the casualty staff.

'I'm flattered,' he said softly. 'I didn't know you cared so much.'

Sarah left him then, for he wanted to stay until the boy's X-ray results came back.

Helen drove her back to Linfield House so that

she could bath and change before the barbecue. After she'd left Casualty she'd gone to check in at the social club where she'd met Lucy and Helen and explained to them what had happened.

Now on the drive home she was mostly silent, weary from exhaustion but overwhelmed by relief.

Helen brought the car to a halt outside Linfield House, and as Sarah opened the door she said, 'Well, if nothing else comes of today, at least you have your proof.'

Sarah paused and looked over her shoulder at Helen. 'Proof of what?'

'Of the strength of your feelings for Liam. I've never seen anything like it. You took off like a bat out of hell when you thought he was in danger. You can't need any more proof than that.'

Sarah smiled sheepishly, climbed from the car, then leaned forward so that she could speak to Helen through the open window. 'I guess you're right—all I need now is proof of the strength of his feelings for me.'

'Does that mean you've decided to break with Gary?' asked her friend.

She hesitated, wondering if she could make Helen understand. 'There wasn't really any need. I had a letter from Gary yesterday—he's decided to stay in Birmingham—so what I had to tell him was much easier than I'd feared. I wrote back and explained that I felt our relationship was at an end.'

'And what about Liam? Does he know that yet?'

Sarah shook her head. 'No, not yet.'

'Well, might I suggest you tell him? Then you

might find out how he really feels about you.' Shaking her head, Helen pulled away, leaving Sarah standing on the kerb watching her.

She soaked for nearly an hour in the bath, relaxing her aching limbs in scented foaming water, then after drying her hair she dressed in a warm Aran jersey and thick cord trousers. There was no sound from Liam's flat, and she guessed he was still at the hospital.

When she finally left the house she could see the glow of the bonfire on the beach beneath the cliffs.

It was a still, calm evening, the sky wide and starlit, and Sarah crossed the road to the beach and the water's edge, preferring to take that route to the barbecue rather than the more conventional one of the esplanade and the cliff-path.

The tide was on its way out, the surf softly lapping, breaking, in swirls of white lace, then retreating, forming runnels and little dark pools of water in the wet sand.

A ship was far out on the horizon, a block of majestically moving lights both exciting and mysterious, but ashore the hotels were in end-of-season darkness, their owners in far-away exotic places.

As she drew nearer to the huge bonfire Sarah felt the warmth from its leaping flames and caught the tantalising aroma of sizzling meat.

Dozens of dark shapes, mere silhouettes against the brightness, flitted about, grouping, breaking and re-forming like characters in some medieval dance, the sound of their chatter and laughter hanging in the smoky evening air. A burst of rock music blared out from some ghetto-blaster, then died away, to be replaced by the sound of someone strumming a guitar.

Several portable barbecues had been set up close to the cliff-face, and catering staff from the hospital were cooking sausages, burgers, chicken legs, kebabs and steaks. Trestle-tables groaned under the weight of hot jacket potatoes, crusty loaves of bread, salads and cans of drink.

Sarah was helping herself to food when she looked up and found Philip at her elbow.

'Hi, Sarah. Did you finish the walk?'

She grinned. 'Just about. How about you?'

He nodded. 'Yes, although we lost our wager with the porters. They finished a good hour ahead of us. Dr O'Neill didn't finish at all. Have you heard about what happened?'

'Yes,' replied Sarah quietly. 'I hope his sponsors will pay up in the circumstances.'

'They ought to. He was jolly brave, I can tell you. I wouldn't have fancied going over that cliff.' Philip bit into his burger.

At that moment Sarah caught sight of Tina on the fringe of the crowd. She appeared to be searching for someone. 'I think Tina's looking for you, Philip.' She touched his arm.

'What?' he turned. 'Oh, yes — right. Thanks.'

Tina began to move towards them, and Sarah edged away. She'd just caught sight of Lucy and Colin, but more importantly she didn't want Tina to find her even talking to Philip, for that evening she felt far from capable of coping with the other girl's insecurities.

Lucy grinned as Sarah approached and raised her can of lager. 'Feeling better now?'

'Yes.' Sarah smiled. 'It's amazing what a hot bath will do for aching bones.'

'Actually I wasn't meaning your bones, I was more concerned about your stress level.' Lucy winked and Colin looked mystified, but Sarah was saved from answering as the first rocket zoomed into the sky and the crowd gasped, then sighed as it exploded into a cascade of red and silver stars.

The firework display was controlled by members of the local fire brigade, and it was while Sarah was watching, her face turned to the sky as one burst of colour was followed by another, that she suddenly felt someone's arms go round her.

She started, stiffened, then relaxed as Liam murmured. 'At last. I didn't think I was going to make it.'

She turned slightly and saw that he had changed and was wearing jeans and a navy blue fisherman's jersey.

'How's the boy?' she asked.

'He has a fractured femur. But the biggest worry is his spine — he fell awkwardly, you see. Gould, the orthopaedic chap, was still operating when I left. If things go badly the lad could end up a paraplegic. I'll phone in later to see how he is. How have things been going here?'

'Fine. We sold all the tickets. The food's really good, everyone seems to be enjoying themselves, and these fireworks are super.' They both watched as a series of green and pink caterpillar-type lights snaked and cracked their way across the sea.

Liam still had his arms round Sarah, and with a sigh she leaned back, resting her head against his shoulder.

'I wish we could go,' he murmured a little later against her ear.

'What do you mean?' Half laughing, she turned her head.

'What I say. I wish we could leave this lot to it and just disappear into the night.'

'That doesn't sound like the organiser of the Body Scanner Appeal talking,' she teased.

'I know,' he agreed through gritted teeth. 'Believe me, that's the only reason we're staying.'

'But I thought you enjoyed these charity functions.'

'In normal circumstances I do,' said Liam.

'And these aren't normal circumstances?'

He merely tightened his grip by way of an answer, but as the evening went on Sarah sensed his increasing impatience as her own anticipation steadily mounted.

At last it was over. The firemen dismantled the wire framework that had been set up for the firework set pieces, the hospital staff cleared the barbecues and collected rubbish in plastic bags, and Liam thanked his team of helpers for all their efforts.

He stood with his arm round Sarah and they watched as the last group left in the Land Rover that had been used to carry equipment to the site, then as the sound of the vehicle faded into the distance and the red tail-lights disappeared he looked up at the sky. 'How beautiful it is now that it's peaceful again. I'm not sure I want to go now. I always feel at one with the elements on a night like this.'

'We don't have to go yet,' Sarah murmured. 'Let's sit a while and enjoy the stillness.'

He took her hand, and they strolled to the base of the cliffs to what was really a natural indentation in the rock, sheltered on three sides but with a clear view of the satiny black water and the wide, starlit sky.

And it was there that Liam's patience finally gave out and he drew her fiercely into his arms, all restraint gone now and with no place for pretence, excuses or recriminations.

Her urgent response must have told him all he wanted to know, as, with all inhibitions swept aside, he drew her down on to the soft sand and in the glow of the dying embers of the forgotten fire concluded what he had started once before.

Their lovemaking was frenzied, a culmination of all the frustrations and restrained desires that had built up since they had met, and as Sarah clung to him, returning his kisses, she knew without any doubt that she had found her soulmate.

Later they strolled back along the beach to Linfield House and let themselves into Sarah's flat. She made mugs of steaming coffee, and while Liam sat on the sofa she stretched out on the rug at his feet. They knew there were things that needed to be said, but both seemed reluctant to speak in case it in some way destroyed the spell that had been woven between them.

In the end it was Liam who broke the silence. 'I suppose really I should apologise again.'

'Should you?' She leaned back against his legs, then turned her head and looked up into his face.

'I'd vowed I wouldn't let that happen until I was absolutely certain it was what you wanted.'

'And weren't you. . .certain it was what I wanted?'

'I thought it was what you wanted once before,' he said softly. 'But it appeared I was wrong.'

'Ah, but it was only a game the last time.'

'Are you saying it wasn't a game this time?' Stretching out his hand, he tangled his fingers in her silky dark hair.

Ignoring his question, Sarah said, 'So what happened to your vow? What made you break it?'

'I wanted you too much,' he replied simply, and she felt a thrill course through her whole body.

He was silent for a while then, but when Sarah would have spoken he leaned forward, silencing her with his fingers against her lips. 'Hear me out, Sarah,' he said softly, 'then, if you have to, tell me to go, but please let me have my say first.'

He paused and glanced round at her sitting-room, a room alive with the very essence of her — her pictures, her books, cushions and posters, vibrant colours, but softly lit by fringed, shaded lamps — then with a sigh he asked, 'Do you remember when I was telling you about my home and about Mary, about how I knew it was wrong with her? How I said

I was convinced I'd know when I met the woman who was right for me?'

She nodded, watching him, loving every line of his face in the soft half-light.

'Well, I was right — I did know her. I knew the first time I met her, when she ran and joined me in the lift and I took her arm to steady her. I knew when I watched her at work, her quiet way with people. I wanted to be near her, to see her every day, to touch her, and even when I knew she belonged to someone else that wanting didn't stop. The certainty was still there; it didn't go away.'

He paused for a moment, then continued, 'We played a game, a crazy game of make-believe, except that for me it wasn't make-believe, it was the real thing. She tried to stop me, to warn me even that I was wasting my time, and I tried again, much as it pained me, to settle for her friendship.

'Then today she showed me how much she cared — I saw it in her eyes when she thought I'd been hurt. Tonight, I simply couldn't have waited a moment longer. What happened between us only confirmed for me what I've known all along.'

As he finished speaking he leaned forward and, lifting her face, covered her lips with his in a kiss that deepened and thrilled her with every passing moment.

In the end it was Sarah who pulled away. 'Liam,' she whispered, 'that was lovely, but it was only half a story.'

'What do you mean?' He frowned.

'My mother always told me that there are two sides to any story.'

'True. . .but. . .'

'Please. . .it's my turn now. Let me explain.'

'If you're going to tell me to go, Sarah, that it's all been a dreadful mistake, then I'd rather just go now. . .'

'Liam, will you please stop for one second and listen?' She was half laughing now, in spite of the seriousness of the moment.

'Very well, I'm sorry. I will.' The soft Irish brogue had never been more pronounced, and Sarah smiled as she gazed into his dark eyes.

'I too was attracted from the moment I met you,' she admitted. 'I admired the way you have with the patients; at first I thought it was simply your Irish charm and that you'd reserve it for certain people, but I quickly realised you were the same to everyone. I was moved by the depth of your compassion, and I was impressed by the tireless way you work for charity. Quite simply, Liam, you fascinated me. I tried not to admit to this attraction even to myself.' She hesitated slightly. 'I was warned that you had the reputation of being a heartbreaker. . .'

'I swear I never——'

'Liam.' There was a warning note in her voice.

'Go on, go on,' he sighed.

'But more important than that was the fact that I was involved in another relationship. I honestly believed that what I had with Gary was the real thing. Even when I knew I was attracted to you I didn't really start to doubt it.'

She paused and glanced at him. 'I'll admit I was shaken by the game we played, and yes, I agree, it was crazy, but it was a chance remark that Lucy made that first caused me to have doubts about Gary.'

Liam half turned then and raised his eyebrows, but Sarah carried on. 'She said I was probably looking forward to him coming home—I know I should have been, but when I thought about it I realised I wasn't. It was then that I began to really examine my feelings for him, and I decided that what both you and Helen had said could be right.'

'What did we say?' queried Liam.

'That sometimes it's a mistake to go back. That people change. I knew then that I'd changed, that my feelings for Gary had changed, and that I had to end our relationship.

Suddenly Sarah realised that Liam had grown very still, almost as if he was holding his breath, waiting for her to go on.

'I dreaded telling Gary, I didn't want to hurt him, but I knew if it went on I'd be living a lie. I decided I'd tell him as soon as he came home, but yesterday I received a letter from him.'

'A letter. . .?'

'Yes. It was the one aspect I hadn't considered, Liam. I realise now that Gary too has changed. He wants something different from life. He's left his father's firm and he's taken a job as a sports instructor in Birmingham. I wrote back to him immediately, but what he'd told me made it much easier to write my letter.'

'Did you tell him about us?' he asked.

'How could I, Liam? Although I felt I knew by then how love really should be, I didn't know for sure how you felt about me. All I did was tell Gary that I felt our relationship had died, that we'd both changed, that we had nothing in common any more, but that I hoped we could remain friends.'

Silence followed as Sarah finished speaking, then she realised that Liam was gazing at her in a kind of stunned wonder as if he couldn't believe what she had just told him.

'But you know now, don't you?' he asked at last.

'Know what?' she asked innocently.

'How I feel about you.'

'Well. . . I think I might need a little more con- vincing——' she began, then gave a little scream as he stood up and pulled her to her feet.

Lifting her into his arms, he carried her into the bedroom, kicking the door shut behind him.

This time he took it slowly, savouring every moment as he undressed her, kissing and caressing every inch of her skin, exploring the secret places of her body and giving undreamed-of pleasure.

And all the while Sarah watched him, delighting in the strong, lean lines of his body as she thrilled to his touch and hungered for that moment when they became one.

But before that he teased, tantalised her, suggest- ing again that it was a game they played.

'No, Liam,' she whispered. 'This time it's for real.'

Fiercely she drew him to her, arching her back to receive him, delighting in the piercing sweetness of the moment, then losing herself in the rhythm of his love as time stood still.

Much later she lay in his arms, drowsy and contented, tracing patterns across the tangle of dark hair of his chest.

'Liam. . .?' she murmured.

'Mmm?'

She lifted her head and looked at him. His eyes were closed. 'I still find it incredible that it was a pure coincidence that you came to live here.'

He didn't answer, neither did he open his eyes, but a smile touched his lips.

'Liam. . .it was a coincidence, wasn't it?' Slowly he opened one eye and grinned at her. She raised herself on to her elbow and looked down at him. 'You said you didn't know I lived here.'

'Was there a name on the advertisement?' he asked.

'No. . .but——'

'Then how could I have known?' The look on his face was one of pure innocence, but the wicked amusement was back in those dark eyes, the look that had captivated her from the very first moment she had seen him.

'I don't know. . .maybe another member of staff told you I lived here.'

'No,' he said solemnly. 'No one told me.' Then, turning to her again, he slid his hand under the duvet and began caressing her, leaving her in no doubt about his immediate intentions.. 'There was no need for anyone to tell me,' he chuckled a moment later.

'What do you mean?' demanded Sarah.

'I watched you pin the advert on the noticeboard.'
She stared at him, then fell on him in mock
exasperation, while he dived beneath the duvet,
pulling her down with him.

4 MEDICAL ROMANCES
AND 2 FREE GIFTS

FROM MILLS & BOON

Capture all the drama and emotion of a hectic medical world
when you accept 4 Medical Romances PLUS a cuddly teddy
bear and a mystery gift - absolutely FREE and without obligation.
And, if you choose, go on to enjoy 4 exciting Medical Romances
every month for only £1.70 each! Be sure to return the coupon
below today to: **Mills & Boon Reader Service, FREEPOST,
PO Box 236, Croydon, Surrey CR9 9EL.**

— — — — — — — | **NO STAMP REQUIRED** | — — — — —

YES! Please rush me 4 FREE Medical Romances and 2 FREE gifts! Please
also reserve me a Reader Service subscription, which means I can look forward
to receiving 4 brand new Medical Romances for only £6.80 every month, postage
and packing FREE. If I choose not to subscribe, I shall write to you within 10
days and still keep my FREE books and gifts. I may cancel or suspend my
subscription at any time. I am over 18 years.
Please write in BLOCK CAPITALS.

Ms/Mrs/Miss/Mr _____ **EP53D**

Address _____

_____

Postcode _____ Signature _____

Offer closes 31st July 1993. The right is reserved to refuse an application
and change the terms of this offer. One application per household. Overseas
readers please write for details. Southern Africa write to B.S.I. Ltd., Box
1654, Craighall, Transvaal 2024. You may be mailed with offers from
other reputable companies as a result of this application. Please tick box if
you would prefer not to receive such offers ☐